David Goodis is ~~~

Passage, Nightfall, ~~~

have been filmed), ~~~ *Corner* and

The Moon in the Gu ~~~

Other Midnight Classics

David Goodis
The Blonde on the Street Corner

Gavin Lambert
Inside Daisy Clover

Horace McCoy
I Should Have Stayed Home
Kiss Tomorrow Goodbye
They Shoot Horses Don't They?
No Pockets in a Shroud

Stewart Meyer
The Lotus Crew

Rudolph Wurlitzer
Flats
Nog
Quake

THE MOON IN
THE GUTTER

David Goodis

**Introduced by
Adrian Wootton**

MIDNIGHT
CLASSICS

Library of Congress Catalog Card Number: 98-86406

A catalogue record for this book is available from
the British Library on request

The right of David Goodis to be identified as
the author of this work has been asserted
in accordance with the Copyright, Designs and
Patents Act 1988

Copyright © The Estate of David Goodis 1983

Introduction copyright © Adrian Wootton 1998

First published in Great Britain by Zomba Books, 1983

First published in this edition, 1998 by Serpent's Tail,
4 Blackstock Mews, London N4

Website: www.serpentstail.com

Set in 10pt NewCenturySchoolbook by Avon Dataset Ltd,
Bidford on Avon

Printed in Great Britain by Mackays of Chatham plc

10 9 8 7 6 5 4 3 2 1

American crime scribe, David Goodis (1917–1967), was the author of some of the most powerful pulp fiction novels to be published in the late 1940s/early 1950s. His work has also been adapted for several classic movies. Yet, as he once said – in typically self-deprecating terms, "I am no Raymond Chandler" and despite the efforts of fans, critics and filmmakers, his work has stubbornly remained a cult treat, resisting every attempt for wider recognition.

The man himself was also a shadowy figure, his relatively short life shrouded in mystery. The known facts, all rounded up in a solitary, still untranslated, French biography, are few and far between. Born in Philadelphia, he had a solid, unspectacular education and, after university, plied his trade as an ad agency copy-writer, whilst literally producing millions of words for pulp short story magazines and contributing scripts to radio serials. His big break and brief glimmer of fame came when his first crime novel, *Dark Passage*, was serialised in *The Saturday Evening Post*, a popular American magazine and, as a result, was bought by Warner Brothers to make into a Bogart and Bacall starring movie. Goodis also gained a contract as a screen-writer out of the deal but, after a few very unsuccessful years in Tinseltown, he rapidly retreated back to his home town of Philadelphia where, living almost entirely

out of the public eye, he churned out one modestly suc-
cessful paperback novel after another until his death in
1967.

In fact, aside from his relatively low-key life-style,
David Goodis's career followed a fairly typical path for a
crime writer of that era. There are similarities between
himself and other notable writers, such as Jim
Thompson. But, unlike Thompson's, the Goodis revival
has never really happened. Perhaps his work is too dark,
too depressing or just too plain sad to attract more than
a small coterie of readers.

Whatever the whys and wherefores of Goodis's obscur-
ity, he is, undoubtedly, a damn fine writer; a unique and
distinctive talent whose best work stands alongside
anything else produced in the crime fiction genre. Goodis
does not tend to write about cops and robbers and he
never created a series character or detective that grew
from one book to the next. Instead, he mined a more
individual – albeit limited – seam of stories set in the
back streets, dumps and dives of urban anytown in the
USA (although all his cities were really Philadelphia
thinly disguised).

David Goodis's characters are occasionally criminals
but this is not terribly important to him. The main thing
for Goodis is the emotional turmoil of life and people who,
for whatever reason, are losers – romantic, twisted,
sometimes exciting, but losers nonetheless, mired in
circumstances from which there is no escape. The titles
of his novels say it all – *Dark Passage*, *Of Missing
Persons*, *Street of the Lost*, *Down There*, *Nightfall* and,
of course, *The Moon in the Gutter*. His men are lonely,
melancholic individuals, often artists who have cracked
up or been in some way irreparably damaged. His

women, on the other hand, veer from the plain, almost saintly sister/good girlfriend through to the sexually rapacious lover/whore. Whilst undoubtedly stereotypes, he invests them with such fierce life that you cannot help but get hooked. Goodis's world view may be despairing and depressing but his writing, replete with hardboiled dialogue and black humour, has – dare one say it – a poetic, almost frightening intensity that makes his stories compulsive page turners.

The Moon in the Gutter, published in 1953, is one of his very finest novels. Written in perhaps the most fertile period of Goodis's career (in the same year as another great Goodis novel, *The Burglar*), it has all the classic components of a definitive Goodis story: a low-life setting, a doomed romance, a man caught between his family and the chance of a new life, a painter on the slide and the typical Goodis references to boxing and be-bop jazz. On publication, it received little or no attention and was just one of many pulp novels bought in newspaper stands throughout the USA. As the years have gone on, however, its reputation has increased and, with the particular assistance of French crime writers and readers, the book has always remained in print there. To be absolutely fair, if it wasn't for French publishers and French directors, Goodis's name may well have disappeared altogether in the 1960s and '70s. The importance of the French Serie Noire crime imprint cannot be underestimated for many crime writers, but particular for Goodis. It was through this that several of the greatest French filmmakers of the last twenty-five years, including Jean Luc Godard and Francois Truffaut, became aware of Goodis and decided to adapt his work for the cinema. Undoubtedly, the most famous of these was Truffaut's classic film version of *Down There*, entitled *Tirez sur le Pianiste* (*Shoot the Pianist*, 1960).

More recently, Jean-Jacques Beineix (the director of such international successes as *Diva* and *Betty Blue*) made his own very expensive and controversial adaptation in 1983 of *Moon in the Gutter*, starring Gerard Depardieu and Nastassia Kinski. Criminally under-rated at the time of release, Beinex's film was not a box office success and so once more Goodis failed to get the attention he deserved. Even so, this loose adaptation of Goodis's work is faithful to the spirit of the novel's world and remains required viewing for anyone interested in the author.

The last – and again, French – film adaptation of David Goodis's work, was nearly a decade ago and, until this Serpent's Tail reissue of *The Moon in the Gutter*, together with *The Blonde on the Street Corner*, there has been little or no publishing interest in Goodis for over ten years. So, maybe this will finally spark that long-lost revival or, at least, introduce him to a new coterie of cult admirers to experience the particular pleasures of Goodisville.

David Goodis's first and only non-crime novel was called, somewhat appropriately, *Retreat from Oblivion* and, thirty-one years on from his death, here's hoping.

CHAPTER 1

At the edge of the alleyway facing Vernon Street, a gray cat waited for a large rat to emerge from its hiding place. The rat had scurried through a gap in the wall of the wooden shack, and the cat was inspecting all the narrow gaps and wondering how the rat had managed to squeeze itself in. In the sticky darkness of a July midnight the cat waited there for more than a half hour. As it walked away, it left its paw prints in the dried blood of a girl who had died here in the alley some seven months ago.

Some moments passed and it was quiet in the alley. Then there was a sound of a man's footsteps coming slowly along Vernon Street. And presently the man entered the alley and stood motionless in the moonlight. He was looking down at the dried bloodstains.

The man's name was William Kerrigan and he was the brother of the girl who had died here in the alley. He never liked to visit this place and it was more on the order of a habit he wished he could break. Lately he'd been coming here night after night. He wondered what made him do it. At times he had the feeling it was vaguely connected with guilt, as though in some indirect way he'd failed to prevent her death. But in more rational moments he knew that his sister had died simply because she wanted to die. The bloodstains were caused by a rusty blade that she'd used on her own throat.

At the time it had happened, he'd been flat on his back in a hospital ward. He was a stevedore, and on the docks a large crate had slipped off its moorings and hit him hard, breaking both his legs. During his third week in the hospital he was told of his sister's suicide.

It was definitely a case of suicide but the circumstances were rather unusual and the authorities decided on a post-mortem examination. They discovered she'd been assaulted. They concluded that she couldn't bear the shock, the shame, and in a fit of despair decided to take her own life.

There were no clues to indicate who had assaulted her. It was the kind of neighborhood where the number of suspects would be limitless. A few were hauled in, questioned, and released. And that was as far as it went.

Seven months ago, Kerrigan was thinking. He stood there looking down at the bloodstains. Attempts had been made to wash them away, and summer rains had thinned them a lot, but the dried red blotches were now a part of the alley paving, stains that couldn't be erased. The moonlight poured on them and made them glisten.

Kerrigan lowered his head. He shut his eyes tightly. His mood was a mixture of sorrow and futile anger. He wondered if the anger would ever find its target. His eyes opened again and he saw the red stains and it was like seeing a permanent question mark.

He sighed heavily. He was a large man, with the accent more on width than on height. He had it mostly in the shoulders, and it amounted to a powerful build composed of hard muscle, two hundred pounds of it, standing five feet ten. His hair was black and thick and combed straight, and he had blue eyes and a nose that had been broken twice but was still in line with the rest of his face. On the left side of his forehead, slanting down towards his cheek, there was a deep jagged scar from an encounter on the docks when someone had used brass knuckles. On the other side, near the corner of his mouth, there was another ridge of healed flesh, from someone's knife. The scars were not at all unique, just a couple of badges that signified he lived on Vernon Street and worked on the docks. Just a stevedore, thirty-five years old, standing here in the dark alley thinking of a dead girl named Catherine.

He was saying to himself: She had the real quality, straight as they come, and it adds up to a damn pity, but you gotta give her credit for what she was, she was born and raised on this street of bums and gin hounds, winos and hopheads, and yet with all that filth around her, she managed to stay clean, through all the twenty-three years of her life.

He sighed and shook his head slowly and started out of the alley. Just then someone called his name and he turned and saw the torn and colorless polo shirt, the slacks that couldn't be patched any more. He saw the sunken-cheeked cadaver, the living waste of time and effort that added up to the face and body of his younger brother.

He said, "Hello, Frank."

"I been lookin' for you."

"For what?" But he already knew. One look at Frank's face and he could tell. He could always tell.

Frank shrugged. "Cash."

He was anxious to get rid of Frank. He said, "How much you need?"

"Fifty dollars."

Kerrigan smiled wryly. "Make it fifty cents."

Frank shrugged again. "All right. That oughta do it." He accepted the silver coin, hefted it in his palm, then slipped it into his trousers pocket. He was twenty-nine. Most of his hair was white. His daily diet consisted largely of five-cent chocolate bars and slot-machine peanuts and as much alcohol as he could pour down his throat. He was fairly gifted at cards and dice and cue sticks, although he'd failed miserably as a purse-snatcher. They hadn't sent him up for it, they'd merely hauled him into a back room at the station house and beat the daylights out of him, and after that he'd stayed away from petty theft. But he was nevertheless proud of his criminal record and he liked to talk about the big operations he'd handle some day, the important deals and transactions he'd manipulate and the territories he'd cover. A long time ago Kerrigan had given up hope that Frank would ever be anything but a booze hound and a corner bum.

"Got a spare weed?" Frank asked.

Kerrigan took out a pack of cigarettes. He gave one to Frank, put one in his own mouth, and struck a match.

He noticed that Frank was gazing past him, the watery eyes aiming down through the darkness of the alley. Frank's expression was thoughtful, then probing, and finally Frank murmured, "You come here often?"

"Now and then."

Frank's eyes narrowed. "Why?"

Kerrigan shrugged. "I'm not sure. I wish I knew."

Frank was quiet for some moments, then he said, "She was a good kid."

Kerrigan nodded.

"One hell of a good kid," Frank said. He took a long drag at the cigarette. He let the smoke come out, and then he added, "Too good for this world."

Kerrigan's smile was gentle. "You know it too?"

They were looking at each other. Frank's face was expressionless. Then his lips twitched and he blinked several times. It seemed he was about to say something. He clamped his mouth tightly to hold it back. The cords of his throat moved spasmodically as he swallowed the unspoken words.

Kerrigan frowned slightly. "What's on your mind?"

"Nothing."

"You look nervous."

"I'm always nervous," Frank said.

"Loosen up," Kerrigan suggested. "Nobody's chasing you."

Frank jerked the cigarette up to his mouth and took a quick draw and bit off some shreds of tobacco and spat them out. He looked off to one side. "Why should anybody chase me?"

"No reason at all," Kerrigan said easily. But inside he felt himself stiffening a little. "That is, unless you've done something."

Frank took a deep breath. He seemed to be staring at nothing. His lips scarcely moved as he said, "Like what?"

"Don't ask me. I don't keep tabs on you."

"You sure you don't?"

"Why should I? You're old enough to look out for yourself."

"I'm glad you know that," Frank said. He straightened his shoulders, trying to look cold and hard. But his lips were twitching, and he went on blinking. He took another conclusive drag at the cigarette and said, "See you later."

Kerrigan watched him as he walked away, crossing

the cobbled surface of Vernon Street and heading towards the taproom on the corner of Third and Vernon. The name of the place was Dugan's Den and it was the only dive in the neighborhood that sold legitimate liquor. All the other joints were in the backrooms of wooden shacks or in the cellars of tenements. Most of the alcohol sold along Vernon Street was home-made and the authorities had long ago given up trying to catch all the bootleggers. Every once in a while there'd be a raid, but it didn't mean anything. They never kept them locked up for long. Just long enough to let them know that pay-offs had to be made on time. So a few days later they'd be back in business at the same old stand.

He stood there at the edge of the alleyway and watched the scarecrow figure of his brother moving towards the murky windows of Dugan's Den. When the fifty cents was used, Frank would hang around Dugan's and beg for drinks, or maybe he'd steal some loose change off the bar and make tracks for the nearest establishment where twenty cents would bring him a water glass filled with rotgut. But there was no point in worrying about Frank.

There was no point in even thinking about Frank. It was a damn shame about Frank, but then, it was a damn shame about a lot of people.

Approaching voices interrupted his thoughts. He looked up and saw the two men. He recognized Mooney, the sign painter. The other man was a construction labourer named Nick Andros. They came up smiling and saying hello, and he nodded amiably. They were men of his own age and he'd known them all his life.

"What's doing?" Nick greeted him.

"Nothing special."

"Looking for action?" Nick asked. He was short and very fat and had a beak of a nose. Totally bald, his polished skull shone in the glow from the street lamps and moonlight.

Kerrigan shook his head. "Just came out to get some air."

"What air?" Mooney grumbled. "Thermometer says ninety-four. We might as well be in a blast furnace."

"There's a breeze coming from the river," Kerrigan said.

"I'm glad you feel it," Mooney said. "For supper I had a plate of ice. Just plain ice."

"That only makes it worse," Kerrigan said. "Try a lukewarm bath."

"I'll hafta try something," Mooney said. "I can't stand this goddamn weather." He was a tall, solidly built man with sloping shoulders and a thick neck. His hair was carrot-colored and he had a lot of it and always kept it combed neatly, parted in the middle and slicked down. His skin was very pale, almost like the skin of an infant. Although he was thirty-six, there were no lines on his face, and his grey-green eyes were clear and bright, so that the only sign of his years was in his voice. He looked more or less like an overgrown boy. Actually, he was a widely-travelled man who'd studied painting in Italy on a fellowship and had been hailed as an important discovery in the art circles of Europe. He'd come back to America to find that his water-colors were acclaimed by the critics but ignored by the patrons. So he'd changed his style in an effort to make sales, and the critics roasted him and then forgot about him. Then everybody forgot about him. He returned to Vernon Street and started painting signs in order to eat. Sometimes when he was drunk he'd talk about his art career, and if he was terribly drunk he'd shout that he was planning another exhibition in the near future. But no matter how drunk he was, he never said nasty things about the critics and the collectors. He never said anything about them one way or another. His primary grudge was against the weather. He was always complaining about the weather.

Nick was laughing. "You shoulda seen him eating the ice. He has a big block of ice on a plate and he's biting it like it's meat or something. He musta et up about ten pounds of ice."

"That's bad for you," Kerrigan told Mooney. "You'll ruin your stomach, doing that."

"My stomach can take anything," Mooney said. "Anything at all. If I can chew it, I can eat it. Last week in Dugan's I won three dollars on a bet."

"Doing what?" Kerrigan asked.

"Eating wood."

Nick nodded. "He actually did it. I was there and I saw him bite the edge off a table and chew it up. Then he swallowed it, the whole mouthful, and he collected three dollars off the slummer."

"Slummer?"

"The playboy," Nick said.

"What playboy?"

"The playboy from uptown," Nick said. "Haven't you seen him?"

Kerrigan shook his head.

"Sure," Nick said. "You musta seen him. He always comes to Dugan's."

Kerrigan shrugged. "I hardly ever go in there, so I wouldn't know."

"Well, anyway, he's one of them playboys who likes to go slumming. One night about a year ago he walked into

Dugan's and now he's one of the regulars. Comes in two, three times a week and drinks himself into a coma. But some nights he only has a few and then he goes out looking for kicks." Nick shook his head solemnly. "A queer proposition if I ever saw one. I've watched him, the way he looks at a woman. Like he ain't satisfied, no matter how much he gets."

"Maybe he ain't getting anything," Mooney commented.

"Maybe," Nick conceded. "But on the other hand, I think he knows how to operate. I got that impression when I offered to get him fixed up. It was something he said when he turned me down."

Kerrigan looked at Nick. "What did he say?"

"He claimed it does nothing for him when he has to pay for it. Paying for it takes away the excitement."

"Maybe he has something there," Mooney said.

"He makes a lot of sense, the way he explains himself," Nick went on. "I asked him if he was married and he said no, he'd tried it a couple times and it always bored him. I guess it's a kind of ulcer in the head that gives him loony ideas."

"You think he's really sick that way?" Kerrigan murmured.

"Well, I'm not an expert in that line."

"The hell you're not," Mooney said.

Nick looked at Mooney. Then he turned again to Kerrigan and said, "I guess most of us are sick with it, one way or another. There ain't a man alive who don't have a problem now and then."

"Not me," Mooney said. "I don't have any problems."

"You got a big problem," Nick told Mooney.

"How come? I got no worries. There's nothing on my mind at all."

"That's your problem," Nick said.

Kerrigan was gazing past them. He said, "I wonder why he comes to Vernon Street."

"Hard to figure," Nick said. "Lotta ways of looking at it. Maybe in his own league he don't rate very high, so he rides down here where he don't hafta look up to anybody."

"Or maybe he just don't like himself," Mooney remarked.

"That's an angle," Nick agreed. Then he frowned thoughtfully. "What it amounts to, I guess, he's probably safer down here."

"Safer?" Kerrigan said.

"What I mean is, he knows he can pull certain stunts on Vernon that he couldn't get away with uptown."

"What kind of stunts?" Kerrigan asked quietly.

"Whatever he has in mind." Nick shrugged. "Who knows what he's gonna dream up? It's a cinch there's something wrong with him, otherwise he wouldn't need this Vernon Street routine."

Kerrigan turned his head slightly and looked into the darkness of the alley behind him.

Then he looked past the heads of Nick and Mooney and focused on Dugan's Den.

He said, "I could use a cold drink."

"I'm dry myself," Nick said.

"Me, I'm dying from thirst," Mooney moaned.

Kerrigan smiled dimly. "I got some loose change. It oughta buy us a few beers."

The three of them started walking towards Dugan's Den. As they crossed the street, Kerrigan turned his head again for a backward glance at the dark alley.

CHAPTER 2

Dugan's Den was twice as old as its proprietor, who was past sixty. The place had never been renovated and it retained its original floor and chairs and tables and bar. All the paint and varnish had vanished long ago, but the ancient wood glimmered with a high polish from the rubbing of countless elbows. Yet, aside from the shiny surfaces of the tables and the bar, Dugan's Den was drab and shabby. It was the kind of room where every time-piece seemed to run slower.

But few of the customers owned watches, and as for the clock on the wall, it wasn't even running at all. At Dugan's there was very little interest in time. They came here to forget about time. Most of them were very old men who had nothing to do and no place to go. And some were white-haired women with no teeth in their mouths and nothing in their heads except the fumes of cheap whisky. The speciality of the house was a double shot of fierce-smelling rye for twenty cents.

There was no jukebox and no television set, and the only entertainment came from Dugan himself. He was a skinny little man with only a few strands of hair on his head and he was always whistling or humming or singing off key. It was a habit he'd developed long ago to keep the place from becoming too quiet. Most of the drinkers were not talkers, and when they did talk it was generally a meaningless jumble of incoherencies that made Dugan wish he were in another line of business. Occasionally there was a loud argument, but it seldom grew to anything really interesting. And on the few occasions when they'd throw fists or bottles, Dugan never made a move to stop them. He led a very monotonous life and he could stand to see a little action now and then.

There were only a few patrons at the bar when Kerrigan came in with Nick and Mooney. Behind the bar, Dugan was dozing standing up, with his arms folded and his chin on his chest. Nick banged his fist on the bar and Dugan opened his eyes and Kerrigan ordered three bottles of beer.

"No bottles," Dugan said, "Ran out of stock late this afternoon. This is a thirsty neighborhood today."

"I'm a thirsty man tonight," Mooney stated. "Let's have it from the tap."

Dugan filled three big glasses and Kerrigan put money on the bar. Behind the bar there was a dirty mirror and he looked in it and saw a man sitting at one of the tables against the wall on the other side of the room. The man had his head lowered to his folded arms on the table and he seemed to be sleeping. Kerrigan noticed that the man was neatly dressed.

"This beer is warm," Mooney was saying.

"There's a shortage of ice," Dugan said.

"You're always short of ice," Mooney complained. "What good is beer if it ain't cold?"

Dugan looked at Mooney. "Did you come in here to raise an issue?"

"I came in to cool off," Mooney said loudly.

"Then cool off," Dugan said. "Just relax and cool off."

"Might as well be drinking hot soup," Mooney

grumbled. "It's a damn shame when a man can't get relief from the heat."

Through the mirror Kerrigan was studying the huddled figure on the other side of the room. He saw that the man had yellow hair cut short, with some silver showing through the yellow. He told himself to stop looking at the man, and he went on looking at him.

"I'm suffocating," Mooney was saying. "It's a goddamn furnace in here. And this beer makes it worse. I feel like I'm melting away to nothing."

A white-haired gin-drinker raised his head from the glass and looked at Mooney. "Why don't you walk down to Wharf Street and jump in the river?"

Nick laughed. But Mooney looked thoughtful, and after a moment he said solemnly, "That ain't a bad idea. Not a bad idea at all."

Mooney turned away from the bar and started out of the taproom. Nick went after him and pulled at his arm.

"Let go," Mooney said. "I need relief from this heat and I'm gonna get it if I have to stay in the river all night."

"It's a cinch you'll stay longer than that," Nick said. "You know you can't swim."

"Well, I'll float." Mooney released his arm from Nick's grasp. He continued toward the door. At the door he turned and looked at Nick and Kerrigan. "You coming with me?"

Nick sighed. "I better be there when you jump in. You'll need someone to pull you out." He went back to the bar and gulped the rest of his beer. Then he looked at Kerrigan. "You coming?"

Kerrigan wasn't listening, and Nick repeated it, and then Nick saw that Kerrigan had his mind on something else. He saw what Kerrigan was looking at in the mirror. Nick's face was expressionless as he watched Kerrigan staring at the mirror that showed the man at the table on the other side of the room. Mooney had already made an exit, and after some moments Nick went to the door and opened it and walked out.

Dugan was dozing again, his head down and his arms folded on his chest as he stood behind the bar and hummed a squeaky tune. The white-haired gin-drinker was gazing tenderly at the few drops remaining in the glass. The other drinkers were bent over the bar and looking at nothing in particular. Then the door of the men's room opened and Frank came out and saw Kerrigan and walked toward him, saying, "What are you doing here?"

Kerrigan took his gaze away from the mirror. He looked at Frank.

"You never come to this place," Frank said. The corner of his mouth went up and came down and went up again. "Why'd you come here tonight? You don't hafta put any tracers on me. I know how to take care of myself. What's your point, anyway? Were you worried how I'd spend your fifty cents?"

"I came here to drink a glass of beer," Kerrigan said.

"Then why don't you drink it?"

Kerrigan lifted the glass to his lips and took a long drink. He put the glass down and Frank was still standing there, breathing hard, the mouth still moving in up-and-down spasms. Frank's eyes were shiny and he was having difficulty standing still.

"What's the matter, Frank?"

"You see anything the matter?"

"Something's on your mind."

"Quit digging." Frank spoke jerkily, as though he'd been running and was out of breath. "You been watching me lately as if you're waiting for some kind of flash news. Every time I look at you, I see you watching me. I'm warning you to lay off."

Kerrigan stood motionless. Frank was moving past him and out of the taproom. He heard a sound that was something like a rumbling roar and it became louder and then he realized it was the dense quiet and stillness that made all the noise. But gradually he was aware of another sound and he concentrated on it, the squeaky little tune that came humming from Dugan's lips. He tried to stay with the music, tried to think of the words that went with the melody, but while his brain moved in that direction his eyes moved to the mirror that showed the man at the table on the other side of the room.

He turned away from the bar and walked slowly toward the table.

He sat down facing the yellow-haired man, who was still slumped over, head buried in folded arms. For almost a full minute he sat there looking at the man. Then he touched the man's wrist and said, "Hey, Johnny, wake up."

"Go away." The man didn't look up. He scarcely moved, except to draw back his wrist from Kerrigan's hand.

"Come on, Johnny. Get with it."

"Leave me alone," the man said.

"Don't you know your old friend Bill?"

The man lifted his head just a little, but his arms still covered his face. He spoke slowly, more distinctly now, measuring his words. "I'm not acquainted with anyone named Bill. And I don't have any old friends."

"But this is Bill Kerrigan. You remember Bill Kerrigan."

"I don't remember anybody," the man said. "I don't like to remember people. All the people I've known I'd rather forget."

"Is it that bad?" Kerrigan wondered if he could really make contact with this man.

"It isn't bad at all," the man said. "It's delightful. It's positively delightful."

"What's delightful, Johnny?"

"The calendar," the man said. "The calendar with the picture of the girl on it. She wore an ermine wrap and it was unbuttoned and she didn't have anything on underneath. That's what I was dreaming about when someone wakes me up and starts calling me Johnny. It so happens my name isn't Johnny."

"What was the name of the girl?"

"What girl?"

"The girl in the dream."

"She didn't have a name," the man said. "None of them have names. They're just a lot of telephone numbers. This one didn't even have a telephone. I like them better when they don't have telephones. And the ones I like best are the dead ones. The dead ones never come around to bother me, not even in dreams."

"But you said it was delightful."

"That's why it bothers me," the man said. "It gets too delightful. It gets so damned delightful that it becomes anguish. Maybe I owe you something for breaking up the dream. You want me to buy you a drink?"

"Sure."

The man raised his head. He had a sallow complexion, and his features were fragile and sensitive. The shadows under his eyes were like a dark reflection of what he had in mind most of the time. He was of average height and weight and he looked to be in his early thirties.

He offered Kerrigan a weary smile. "What are you drinking?"

"I'll have a beer, Johnny."

The smile became dim and sort of sad. "You still think it's Johnny?" He didn't wait for a reply. He got up and went to the bar. Kerrigan watched him as he stood there talking quietly to Dugan. Then he was back at the table with the beer, and a water glass half filled with whisky for himself.

Kerrigan raised his glass. "Good luck, Johnny."

"There's no such thing," the man said. "It's all bad." He grinned at the whisky. Then he took a big gulp of it. He had trouble getting it down and he tried to curse while he was coughing and began to choke. He put a stop to that with another gulp. While it went down he had his eyes shut tightly. Then he was grinning again and he said, "You're lonesome too, aren't you?"

"Sometimes," Kerrigan said.

"I'm lonesome all the time." The man stopped grinning and gazed at the whisky in the glass. "I've been everywhere, I've done everything, and I've known everybody. And what it amounts to, I'm lonesome."

"Maybe you need a woman," Kerrigan ventured.

The man didn't even seem to hear it.

Then it was quiet for some moments and finally the man grinned again and said, "Who are you?"

Kerrigan decided to play it straight. He said, "I'm sorry, mister. I knew I'd never seen you before. It's just that I wanted company. I'm Bill Kerrigan."

"And I'm Newton Channing. Ever hear of Newton

Channing? Does the name mean anything?"

Kerrigan shook his head.

Channing said, "You know, it means nothing to me, either."

There was a long silence. Kerrigan took a sip of beer, and then he said, "Where do you live?"

"Uptown," Channing answered absently. And as he went on talking, it was obvious that his thoughts had nothing to do with what he was saying. "Nice clean neighborhood. Too goddamn clean. Strictly middleclass. House and garage and a lawn in front. I live there with my sister. Just the two of us. She's a nice girl and we get along fairly well. One night last week she knocked me cold."

Kerrigan didn't say anything.

"She's really a very nice girl," Channing said. He lifted the glass to his mouth and finished the whisky. Then he got up from the table and went to the bar and came back with another beer and a pint bottle of whisky. Pouring the whisky, he went on in the detached tone, "I was trying to set fire to the house and she used the heel of her shoe on my head. I was out for at least ten minutes."

"Well, there's nothing like a happy home."

Channing filled the water glass to the brim. He lifted the glass very carefully and drank the whisky as though he were drinking water. He consumed more than a third of the glass before he said, "You know, I admire my sister. I really do. Only thing I object to, she has some notion I can't take care of myself. It makes her maternal. Lately she's been coming here to pick me up and drive me home."

"Can't you make it alone?"

Channing shrugged. "Usually I'm too drunk to handle

a car. When that happens, Dugan calls for a taxi. I don't like to see my sister coming down here. I'd much rather go home in a taxi."

"It's a lot safer," Kerrigan said. "I mean, it's safer for your sister. After all, this is a rough neighborhood."

"She doesn't care about that."

"The point is," Kerrigan said, "it's a very rough neighborhood and it's especially bad for a woman."

Channing inclined his head and gave Kerrigan a side glance. "Maybe you're just sitting here and pulling my leg."

Kerrigan didn't reply.

"Something bothers you," Channing said. "You're not chatting with me just to pass the time." He leaned forward, and his gaze was intent. "What's really on your mind?"

"Nothing special," Kerrigan said.

Channing drank more whisky. He kept the glass in his hand and stared at it. "Maybe you're a mugger. Maybe you're building up to some clever dodge. Like getting me alone somewhere and knocking my brains out and taking my wallet."

"Could be," Kerrigan agreed. "In a neighborhood like this, you never know who you're dealing with. It's always smart to be careful."

Channing laughed softly. "My friend, let me tell you something. I don't give a damn what happens to me."

Kerrigan watched him as he finished the whisky in the glass and lifted the bottle to pour some more. The glass was filled again and Channing had it almost half empty when there was the sound of a door opening and Kerrigan looked up and saw the woman coming into Dugan's Den.

She was walking toward the table. She moved slowly, casually, with a certain poise that blended with her face and body. She had a very beautiful face and her figure was slender and elegant. She had long wavy hair and greenish eyes. Her height was around five-four and she appeared to be in her middle twenties.

But he wasn't thinking about her age. He wasn't exactly sure what he was thinking. He could feel the tingling fascination of her physical presence and at the same time he was irritated with himself for staring at her.

He didn't realize that she was returning his stare. Whatever her reaction was, she did a nice job of hiding it. It lasted that way for a few minutes or so, then she was looking at her brother and saying, "All right, Newton. Finish your drink and let's go home."

Channing smiled at the whisky glass. "I ought to pay you a salary. What are nursemaids getting these days?"

"It isn't that kind of job." Her tone was quiet and amiable. "It isn't a job at all. I don't mind it in the least."

Channing shrugged. "You might as well sit down and have a drink. I'm not ready to go yet. I still have some drinking to do."

"How much have you had?"

"Very little, really."

"That means you've had almost a quart."

"It hasn't hit me yet," Channing said. "I've got to stay here until it hits me."

"One of these nights it'll really hit you and you'll be carried out on a stretcher." She was looking down at her brother as though examining a curious exhibit. "I'm absolutely certain you'll wind up in a hospital. Is that what you want?"

"I want you to leave me alone." He looked up at her, smiling faintly. "I hope it's not asking too much, but I'd really be grateful if you'd leave me alone."

"I can't do that," she said. "I'm much too fond of you."

"That's awfully sweet," Channing said. He looked at Kerrigan. "Don't you think that's sweet? Wouldn't you say I'm fortunate to have such a nice sister?"

Kerrigan was silent.

He heard her saying, "You're not polite, Newton. You ought to introduce your friend."

"By all means," Channing said. Then, to no one in particular, "Please forgive my bad manners." He half stood and waited for Kerrigan to stand. But Kerrigan sat there. Channing shrugged, lowered himself to the seat, and poured more whisky into the glass. Then he went to work on the whisky.

"I'm still waiting," she said. "I'm waiting for the introduction."

"Oh, the hell with it." Channing took a big gulp of whisky. "As a matter of fact, the hell with everything."

She looked at Kerrigan. She said, "I'm sorry. He doesn't really mean that. It's just that he's drunk."

"It's all right."

She studied Kerrigan's face. "Please don't be offended."

He spoke a trifle louder. "I said it's all right."

"Sure it's all right," Channing said. "Why shouldn't it be all right?"

She looked at Channing. "You be quiet," she said. "Just sit there and drink your whisky and don't say anything. You're in no condition to say anything."

Channing sat up stiffly. He stared off to the side, his eyes focused on nothing. "What do you know about my condition?"

She didn't bother to answer. She turned to Kerrigan. "May I introduce myself? I'm Loretta Channing."

"That means a lot to him," Channing said. "It's very important that he should know your name. Why don't you give him your address? Tell him he's welcome any time. Invite him to dinner."

She went on looking at Kerrigan.

And Channing said, "He doesn't think you mean it. You've got to make it more sincere. Don't stand there looking down at him. Sit beside him."

"I told you to be quiet."

"Go on, sit beside him. Take hold of his hand."

"Will you shut your mouth?"

Channing was laughing. "Prove it to him, let him know you're on the level. Maybe you'll convince him if you drink from his glass."

"Maybe I'll slap your face," she told Channing. "You're not too drunk to get your face slapped."

Channing went on laughing. It was almost soundless laughter and gradually it subsided and became a series of little gasps, more like sobs. He made a grab for the glass and tossed more whisky down his throat. Then he turned so that he faced the wall. He sat there drinking and staring at the wall as though he were in a room alone with himself.

She was looking at Kerrigan, waiting for him to tell her his name.

He swallowed hard. "My name is Kerrigan." He said it through his teeth. "William Kerrigan. I live right here on Vernon Street. The address is five-twenty-seven."

Then he got up from the table, and he was facing her and standing close to her. There was a heaviness on his chest and it caused him to breathe hard.

He said, "Got it straight? It's five-twenty-seven Vernon." He was trying to say it calmly and softly, with velvety sarcasm, but his voice trembled. "You're welcome to visit there any time. Come over some night for dinner."

She winced and took a backward step. He moved past her and headed for the door and walked out.

As he hit the street he felt better, remembering the way she'd winced. It wasn't much, but it was something. It offered a little satisfaction. But all at once she faded from his mind and everything faded except the things in front of his eyes, the rutted street and the gutter and the sagging doorsteps of decaying houses.

It struck him full force, the unavoidable knowledge that he was riding through life on a fourth-class ticket.

He stared at the splintered front doors and unwashed windows and the endless obscene phrases inscribed with chalk on the tenement walls. For a moment he stopped and looked at the ageless two-word phrase, printed in yellow chalk by some nameless expert who'd put it there in precise Gothic lettering. It was Vernon Street's favorite message to the world. And now, in Gothic print, its harsh and ugly meaning was tempered with a strange solemnity. He stood there and read it aloud.

The sound was somehow soothing. He managed to smile at himself. Then he shrugged, and turned away from the chalked wall, and went on walking down Vernon Street.

CHAPTER 3

He walked slowly, not with weariness, but only because he didn't feel quite ready to go home and he wanted the walk to last as long as possible. From a small pocket in his work pants he took out a nickel-plated watch and the dial showed twenty past one. He wondered why he wasn't sleepy. On the docks today he'd put in three hours' overtime and he'd been up since five in the morning. He knew he should have been in bed long ago. He couldn't understand why he wasn't tired.

He moved past the vacant lots on Fourth Street and walked parallel to a row of wooden shacks where the colored people lived. One of the shacks contained a still that manufactured corn whisky. The bootlegger's neighbors were elderly churchgoing people who continually reported the bootlegger to the authorities, and were unable to understand why the bootlegger was never arrested. The bootlegger could have told them that he always handed his payoffs to the law when his neighbors were in church. It simplified matters all round.

Bordering the wooden shacks there was an alley, then another vacant lot, then a couple of two-storied brick tenements filled with Armenians, Ukranians, Norwegians, Portuguese, and various mixed breeds. They all got along fairly well except on week ends, when there was a lot of drinking, and then the only thing that could stop the commotion was the arrival of the Riot Squad.

Passing the tenements, he crossed another alley and arrived at the three-storied wooden house that was almost two hundred years old. It was owned by his father and it had been handed down through four generations of Kerrigans.

He stood there on the pavement and looked at the house and saw the loose slats and the broken shutters and the caved-in doorsteps. There was only a little paint clinging to the wooden walls and it was chipped and had long ago lost its color, so that the house was a drab, unadorned gray, a splintered and unsightly piece of rundown real estate, just like any other dump on Vernon Street.

The Kerrigans occupied only the first floor; the two upper floors were rented out to other families, who were always bringing in more relatives. There was really no way to determine how many tenants were upstairs. From the noise they usually made, it sometimes seemed to Kerrigan that he was living underneath a zoo crammed to the limit with wild animals. But he knew he had no right to complain. The first floor did all right for itself when it came to making noise.

He opened the front door and walked into a dimly lit parlor that featured a torn carpet, several sagging chairs, and an ancient sofa with most of the stuffing falling out of the upholstery. His father, Tom, was sound asleep on the sofa, but he awakened and sat up when Kerrigan was halfway across the room.

Tom Kerrigan was fifty-three, an extremely good-looking man with a carefully combed pure-white pompadour, a tall and heavy and muscular body, and absolutely no ambition. At various times in his life he had shown considerable promise as an Irish tenor, a heavy-weight wrestler, a politician and a salesman and a real-estate agent. He might have attained the heights in any of these fields, but he was definitely a loafer, and the more he loafed, the happier he appeared to be. As he sometimes put it, "It's a short life and there ain't no sense in knocking yourself out."

Sitting on the edge of the sofa, Tom let out a tremendous yawn, and then he smiled amiably at his son. "Just coming in?"

Kerrigan nodded. "Sorry I woke you up."

Tom shrugged. "I didn't feel like sleeping anyway. This goddamn sofa was breaking my back."

"What's wrong with your bedroom?"

"Lola threw me out."

"Again?"

Tom frowned and rubbed the back of his neck. "I don't know what the hell's wrong with that woman. She's always been an evil-tempered hellcat, but lately she's been carrying on something fierce. I swear, she tried to murder me tonight. Threw a table at me. If I hadn't ducked, it would've knocked my brains out."

Kerrigan sat down in a chair near the sofa. He sensed that his father was in a talkative mood, and he was perfectly willing to sit here and listen. Somehow he always felt relaxed and content when he was alone with Tom. He liked Tom.

"Let me tell you one thing," Tom said. "It ain't no cinch living with a woman like that. It's like playing around with a stick of dynamite. The thing that beats the hell out of me is why I stay here and take it." Tom shook his head slowly and sighed.

Kerrigan shifted his position in the chair. He settled

back halfway against the wooden arm and flung both legs over the other arm.

Tom said, "It's always something. Last week she claims I'm monkeying around with some woman lives upstairs. Now for God's sake, I ask you man to man, would I do a thing like that?"

"Of course not," Kerrigan murmured, and checked it off as a lily-white lie. Tom had quite a reputation in the neighborhood.

"You're damn right I wouldn't," Tom declared. "When I marry a woman, I stay faithful to her. If I say so myself, I think I'm one hell of a good husband. I was good to your mother and after she died I was loyal to her memory for three entire years. For three years, mind you, I wouldn't let myself look at a skirt. Now that's the truth."

Kerrigan nodded solemnly.

"Come to think of it," Tom said, "your mother wasn't so easy to live with, either. But let her rest in peace. She was an awful nag, but she wasn't so bad compared to these other wives I've had. Like that second one, that Hannah. I swear, that woman was completely out of her mind. And the next one I married, that Spanish woman. What was her name?"

"Conchita."

"Yes," Tom said. "Conchita. She was one hot tomato, but I didn't like that knife she carried. It bothers me when they carry a knife. That's one thing I can say for Lola. She never reaches for a knife."

"Why'd she heave the table at you?"

Tom sighed heavily. "We had a discussion about the rent. She claims the tenants upstairs are four months behind."

"She's right about that," Kerrigan murmured. "It adds up to more than a hundred dollars."

"I know," Tom admitted. "And we sure can use the cash. But I just don't have the heart to put the pressure on them. Can't squeeze money out of people when they don't have it. Old Patrizzi ain't worked for a year. And Cherenski's wife is still in the hospital."

"What about the others?"

"They're all up the same creek. Last time I went upstairs to make collections, I heard so much grief it gave me the blues and I stayed drunk for three days."

From one of the other rooms there was the sound of a door opening, then heavy footsteps approached through the hall. Kerrigan looked up to see Lola entering the parlor. She was a huge woman in her middle forties, with jet-black hair parted in the middle and pulled back tightly behind her ears. Weighing close to two hundred pounds, she had it distributed with emphasis high up front and in the rear, with an amazingly narrow waist and long legs that made her five feet nine seem much taller. She moved with a kind of challenge, as though flaunting her hips to the masculine gender and letting them know she was the kind of woman they had to fight for. The few who had dared had wound up with badly lacerated faces, for Lola was an accomplished mauler and she'd been employed as a bouncer in some of the roughest joints along the docks.

Her complexion was dark, and some Cherokee red showed distinctly when she was riled. Actually the Cherokee was mixed with French and Irish, with accent on the more explosive traits of each.

Lola moved toward the sofa, her hands on her hips, directing her full attention to Tom. Her booming lower-octave voice was like the thud of a heavy cudgel as she said, "You gonna go upstairs and collect that rent?"

"Now look, sweetheart. I told you—"

"I know what you told me. It's for the birds, what you told me. You're gonna get that money and you're gonna get it tonight."

"But they don't have it. They swore to me—"

"They're nothing but a bunch of goddamn liars," Lola shouted. "I'd go up there myself and make them pay off or get the hell out, but that ain't my department. You're the owner of this house and it's your job to deal with the tenants."

"Well, after all, I've been busy."

"Doing what?" Lola demanded. "Sitting on your rear all day and drinking beer? That's another thing I'm fed up with. Morning, noon and night it's beer, beer, beer. We got enough empty bottles in the back yard to start a glass factory."

"The doctor says it's good for my stomach."

"What doctor? What are you giving me? When you been to see a doctor?"

"Well, I didn't want to worry you."

Lola moved closer to the sofa and pointed a thick finger in Tom's face. "You're so goddamn healthy it's a downright disgrace. Why shouldn't you be healthy? All you do is eat and sleep and drink beer. If it wasn't for your son here bringing in the pay check, we'd all be living on relief."

Tom assumed a hurt look. "Is it my fault if times are hard?"

"It ain't the times, and you know it. If anyone came and offered you a job, you'd drop dead, you'd be so scared." As though addressing a roomful of spectators, she indicated Tom with an extended palm and said, "I tell him to go upstairs and get the rent money and he claims it wouldn't be charitable." She whirled on Tom and yelled, "Where do you come off with that charity routine? You're just too goddamn lazy to climb a couple flights of stairs."

"Now look, sweetheart—"

Lola cut in with another burst of condemnation, spicing it with oaths and four-letter words. The walls of the parlor seemed to vibrate with the force of her loud harangue. Kerrigan knew from past experience that it would go on like this for the better part of the night. He walked out of the parlor and moved slowly down the narrow hallway leading to the small bedroom he shared with Frank. But all at once he stopped. He was looking at the door of another room. It was an empty room and no one lived in it now and he wondered what caused him to stare at the door.

He tried to drag his eyes away from the door, but even while making the effort he was putting his hand on the knob. He opened the door very slowly and went in and flicked the wall switch that lit the single bulb in the ceiling. He closed the door behind him and stood looking at the walls and the floor, the bed and the chair, the small dresser and tiny table. He was thinking of the girl who had lived here, the girl who'd been dead for seven months.

Without sound he spoke her name. Catherine, he said. And then he was frowning, annoyed with himself. It didn't make sense to sustain the sorrow. All right, she'd been his sister, his own flesh and blood, she'd been a fine sweet tenderhearted creature, but now she was gone and there was no way to bring her back. He tried to shrug it off and walk out of the room. But something held him there. It was almost as though he were waiting to hear a voice.

Then suddenly he heard it, but it wasn't a voice. It was the door. He turned slowly and saw Frank coming into the room.

They looked at each other. Frank's mouth was twitching. The eyes were very shiny, the arms hanging stiffly and the hands slanted out at an odd angle with the fingers stretched rigid. Then Frank was staring at the wall behind Kerrigan's head and saying quietly, "What goes on here?"

Kerrigan didn't reply.

"I'm asking you something," Frank said. "Whatcha doing in this room?"

"Nothing."

"You're a liar," Frank said.

"All right, I'm a liar." He made a move toward the door. Frank wouldn't get out of the way.

"I want to know what you're up to," Frank said. He blinked a few times. "We might as well get it straight here and now."

"Get what straight?" Kerrigan's eyes were drilling the face in front of him and trying to see what was going on in Frank's mind.

Frank began to breathe very fast. Again he was staring at the wall. He said, "You're not fooling me. You got a long way to go before you can fool me."

Kerrigan made a weary gesture. "For God's sake," he said. "Why don't you knock it off? Quit looking for trouble."

Frank blinked again, and then for a moment his eyes were tightly shut as though he were trying to erase something from his mind. Whatever it was, it wouldn't go away, and the weight of it seemed to push down on him, causing his skinny shoulders to sag. His head was bent low, and light from the ceiling bulb put a soft glow on his white hair. There was something gloomy in the way the light fell on him. It was like an eye looking down at him, feeling sorry for him.

It occurred to Kerrigan that he ought to show kindness toward Frank. He sensed that Frank was headed toward a breakdown, the total result of too many bad habits, especially alcohol. He thought, poor devil looks all washed out, just about ready to drop.

He smiled softly and reached out and put his hand on Frank's shoulder. Frank hopped backward as though he'd been jabbed with a hot needle. And then he went on moving backward, crouching and breathing fast with his mouth opened so that his teeth showed. His trembling lips released the choked whisper, "Keep your hands off me."

"I'm only trying—"

"You're trying to ruin me," Frank gasped. "You won't be satisfied until I'm all smashed up, done for, finished. But I won't let you do it. I won't let you." His voice went up to a thin wail that twisted and snapped and then he was staring at floor and walls and ceiling, like a trapped creature frantically seeking escape.

"Want a cigarette?" Kerrigan said.

Frank didn't seem to hear. His lips were moving without sound and it appeared he was talking to himself.

Kerrigan lit a cigarette for himself and stood there watching as Frank sat down on the edge of the bed and lowered his head into his arms. Kerrigan thought. It ain't that he's afraid of me, it's got nothing to do with me, he's afraid of the world, he's finally got to the point where he can't face the world.

He heard Frank saying dully, "I want you to leave me alone."

"I'm not bothering you, Frank. Seems to me it's the other way around."

"Just lay off. That's all I ask."

"Sure, Frank." His voice was as soft and gentle as he could make it. "That's what I've been doing all along. I've never stood in your way. Whatever you do is your own affair."

Frank stood up. He was calmer now, he seemed to have control of himself. But as he moved toward the door, he wasn't looking at Kerrigan. It was as though Kerrigan weren't there.

When Frank had gone, Kerrigan took a long drag from the cigarette. He went on dragging at it until it was down to a stub that scorched his fingers. He hurled the stub to the floor and stepped on it.

Suddenly he felt smothered in here. And somehow it had nothing to do with the tobacco smoke that filled the room. He made a lunge for the doorknob, telling himself that he needed air.

He hurried through the hall and across the parlor. He opened the front door, came out on the doorstep, and saw the other female member of the household. Her name was Bella and she was Lola's daughter. She was sitting on the top step, and as she sensed his presence, her head turned very slowly, and her eyes drilled him with a mixture of icy scorn and fiery need.

CHAPTER 4

"Hello," Kerrigan said.

"You go to hell."

"Still mad at me?"

"Do me a favor. Drink some poison."

Bella was in her middle twenties. She'd been married three times, once by a judge and twice by common law. Somewhat tall and on the plump side, she was a slightly smaller edition of her mother. Her hair was the same jet black, her eyes dark and flashing, her complexion a Cherokee russet. She had the same generously rounded build as Lola, and emphasized it with tightly fitting blouses and skirts.

She had a loud and very bushy mouth, an evil temper, and she wasn't afraid of a living soul with the exception of her mother. Some weeks ago, during an argument in the parlor, she'd kicked Kerrigan and really hurt him, and Lola grabbed her and tore her up so badly with an ironing cord that she couldn't leave the house for two days.

Kerrigan smiled at her. "What's the gripe this time?"

"Take a walk," Bella snapped. "I told you a week ago you're off my list."

He sat down beside her on the doorstep. "I still don't know what you're sore about."

Bella stared straight ahead. "You got a short memory, mister."

Somehow tonight he found her presence invigorating and her nearness gave him a feeling of comfort and pleasure.

He said, "I think it was something about a blonde."

She scowled. "Can't you remember which one? Maybe you got so many on the string, you forget their names."

"Was it Vera?"

"No, it wasn't Vera. And while we're at it, who the hell is Vera?"

Kerrigan shrugged. "She's a waitress. When I'm in a diner I gotta talk to the waitress. I gotta tell her what I wanta eat."

Bella didn't reply. Kerrigan offered her a cigarette and she grudgingly accepted. He pulled a book of matches from his trousers pocket and lit it. For a while they sat there just smoking.

Finally Bella said, "It wasn't no waitress I saw you with. To me she looked like a two-dollar type. You took her for a walk up Second and then you went in a house with her."

"What house? What are you talking about?" He frowned with genuine bewilderment and rubbed the back of his head. Then, as the incident came back, "For God's sake, that was no house, it was a store. She's married and has five children. Her husband sells secondhand furniture. I told her we needed another lamp for the parlor. If you don't believe me, go inside and take a look. You'll see the lamp I bought."

Bella was convinced, but not mollified. She said, "Why didn't you tell me that when I asked you the first time?"

"I didn't like the way you asked me, that's why. Didn't even give me a chance to explain. Just came leaping at me like a wildcat."

"Did you have to punch me in the face?"

"If I hadn't, you'd have torn my eyes out."

"One of these days I will."

He showed her an easy grin. "Don't do it when your mother's around."

"She won't stop me the next time. Nothing will."

Kerrigan let the grin fade. He didn't like the look on Bella's face. There was a grimness in her eyes that made him know she meant every word she said.

"What's the big beef?" he said. "What's eating you?"

For a moment she was quiet. Then she said, "I'm tired of waiting."

"Waiting? For what?"

Her eyes drilled him. "You know."

He looked away from her. "Hell," he muttered. "Are we gonna start that again?"

"I want it settled once and for all," Bella said. "We getting married or ain't we?"

He took a final pull at the cigarette and flipped it into the street. "I don't know yet."

"What do you mean, you don't know? What's holding you back?"

He groped for an answer, and couldn't find any. His shoulders were hunched, his folded arms pressing on his knees as he scowled at the pavement.

"Why shouldn't we get married?" Bella demanded. "We go for each other, don't we?"

"It needs more than that."

"Like what?"

Again he couldn't provide an answer.

"Where's the complication?" Bella wanted to know. "We're living in the same house, we eat at the same table. It ain't as if you gotta make some major changes. All we do is kick Frank out of your room and put him in mine. Then I bring my clothes across the hall and we're all set."

His scowl deepened. He tried to say something but his lips wouldn't move.

She inclined her head slightly, studying him with open suspicion. "Maybe you got some other plans that don't include me."

He didn't reply. He had the vague notion she'd spoken an important truth that he couldn't admit to himself.

Bella said, "Whatever you do, don't play me cheap. I ain't in the market for any raw deals."

He frowned at her. "You're too jealous."

She didn't say anything for some moments. Then, very quietly, "I got every right to be jealous."

His eyes flared, his voice climbed. "Whatcha want me to do, lock myself up in a closet?"

"I wish you would." She wasn't looking at him. She stared at the cobbled street as though its lifeless stillness were the only audience for her deeper thoughts. "What is it with me?" she murmured. Then, moving her head slightly to indicate Kerrigan, "I got this guy in my blood like a disease. It's reached the point where I can't think about anything else."

Kerrigan gaped at her. For the first time he was fully aware of Bella's great need for him, the extent of her want, which went far beyond the physical drive. He had long known that she was genuinely attracted to him, and her behavior on the mattress was always sufficient proof that he gave her something special. But he'd never anticipated that her hunger for him would become the major factor in her life. He realized now that he'd been taking Bella for granted, that although he always looked forward to being with her, he'd never had the deeper feeling, the feeling she was now expressing toward him.

Suddenly he sensed that he'd been giving Bella a bad time. His eyes clouded with guilt. He wanted very much to say something affectionate and reassuring, but he couldn't find the phrases.

She was looking at him. She was saying, "Some nights in bed I sit up wide awake, trying to figure out what it is with me and you. For some crazy reason I keep having a dream where I see you standing on top of a mountain. I'm somewheres around, just where I don't know. And there's a hundred thousand other women reaching up to get you. For months now I've been having that same dream."

Kerrigan smiled gently. "Don't let it bother you. You got no competition."

"If only I could believe that."

"I'm saying it, ain't I?"

"Saying it ain't enough." There was worry in her eyes, and her voice was dull and heavy with doubt. "I just can't get rid of this jealous feeling. Why should it hit me so hard?"

He shrugged. "Beats the hell out of me. All I know is, I haven't messed with any other skirt since you and me got started."

It was evident that she believed him. And yet the worry stayed in her eyes. "It's not that I'm imagining things. And it ain't the way you look at women, either. It's the way they look at you. Even when they're on the other side of the street and you come walking past, I see them turning their heads. I know just what's in their minds."

He shrugged again. "These Vernon dames'll look twice at anything wearing pants."

"No, they won't," she said. "I'm one of them, I ought to know. It's just that there's something about you that women go for."

There was nothing complimentary in the way she said it. Her tone was sullen and resentful. "I'll be damned if I know what makes them so weak for you. After all, what are you? Just a big chunk of beef, an ordinary dock-walloper who never even finished high school. And you sure as hell ain't pretty. I've seen punch-drunk pugs who could give you cards and spades and come out in front. So I know it ain't looks. And it ain't brains. I wish to God I could figure out what it is."

Kerrigan was vaguely uncomfortable and somewhat annoyed with this probing of his physical and mental make-up. "Don't knock yourself out trying to figure me. Just relax and take me as I am."

For a long moment she just sat there and looked at him. Then gradually her lips shaped a smile, the sparks came into her eyes, and the red of her cheeks grew redder.

She stood up and said, "Come on, let's go in."

He started to move. But something kept him seated there on the doorstep. He frowned slightly and said, "I want to sit here for a while."

"How long?"

"Just a few minutes."

"All right," she said. "But don't make it longer. I don't feel like waiting."

He heard the door opening and closing behind him, and told himself that he was alone now. It was as though a weight had been lifted from his shoulders. But at the same time he wondered why he was thinking in terms of a burden instead of enjoyment.

As he sat there gazing moodily at the pavement, there was the purring sound of an automobile approaching at low speed. He looked up and saw an open-top sport car gliding toward the curb.

He winced, then stiffened, staring at the golden hair of Loretta Channing.

CHAPTER 5

The sport car came to a stop directly in front of the
Kerrigan house. Loretta climbed out and walked toward
him. He winced again, trying to ignore a strange stir of
excitement. Gradually he managed to get a sullen look
in his eyes. And he could feel his resentment growing
when he saw how relaxed she was. As she came up to
him, he muttered, "You sure you got the right address?"

She nodded. She wasn't smiling. "I'm accepting your
invitation."

"It's a little late for dinner."

"I didn't come for dinner."

He sat there on the doorstep and scowled at her.

She said offhandedly, "It's just a visit. Just felt like
seeing you."

"That's nice." He gazed past her. "You make a habit of
calling on people at two-thirty in the morning?"

She shrugged lightly. "I was hoping you wouldn't be
asleep."

"If I was, you'd probably wake me up. Maybe you'd
force the door open and break into my room."

"Not really," she said. "I never take it that far."

He gave her a side glance. "I'm not so sure about that."

It was quiet for a few moments. Then she said, "Like
to go for a ride?"

It caught him off guard. He frowned at her, his eyes
asking questions that were aimed mostly at himself.

She said, "It's a perfect night for a ride." She pointed backward to the car. "The top is down and we'll get a breeze. Nice way to cool off."

Before he realized what he was doing, he stood up and followed her to the car. It was a pale gray MG with yellow leather upholstery.

She climbed in behind the wheel. He stood there hesitantly. Then he saw her looking at him. She was smiling. It was a dim smile, like a dare. He had the feeling he was bracing himself for a test. His teeth were clenched as he walked around to the other side of the car.

He opened the door. He started to climb in and then he stopped and said, "This is very nice upholstery. You sure I won't get it dirty? I'm wearing my working clothes."

"Please get in."

She was starting the engine. He got in and settled back in the seat. The car moved away from the curb. They took a corner and then another corner and the MG came back onto Vernon. She wasn't pushing it, just letting it glide. He settled back and told himself to enjoy the cruise. The hell with her. It was a nice hunk of automobile and it was giving him a smooth ride and that was all. But then he wondered if his grimy trousers were dirtying the upholstery. He bit at the side of his mouth.

Then he noticed they were headed in the direction of Wharf Street and he said, "We're going toward the docks."

"Yes, I know."

"You been here before?"

"Many times," she said. "But I've never seen the river at night. Do you mind if we have a look at it?"

He shrugged. "You're the driver."

The MG came onto Wharf Street and turned left and moved parallel to the docks. They were going very slowly now, cruising past the hulking shadowy shapes of piers and warehouses. In the black water along the wharves the big freighters were settled like motionless oxen waiting for morning. Within another hour the river activity would begin, the trucks would arrive to receive cargo from incoming ships, and workers would be straining under the weight of bales and crates and heavy cardboard boxes. But now, in the moonlight, the piers were deserted, and the only sound was the engine of the MG.

The car made a sudden and unexpected turn. He saw she was taking it onto the planks of a wide pier. On one side of the pier there was a big Dutch tanker, and the other side showed the suspension bridge that spanned the river like a huge curved blade of silver in the black sky. In front, the edge of the pier gave way to a couple of miles of deep water, its blackness streaked and dotted with the reflection of city lights. It was like millions of varicolored sequins on black satin.

They were parked at the edge of the pier and she was gazing out at the river. "It's breathtaking."

He didn't know what she meant. He looked at her.

She moved her hand to indicate the river and the sky and the ships and the bridge. "It's really magnificent."

He grunted. "Well, that's one way of looking at it." Then, with a shrug, "I guess it's a nice view for the sightseers."

"Why do you say that? Don't you think it's a nice view?"

"Maybe I'd think so if I didn't work here." He gazed down at the calloused palms of his hands. It was quiet for a long moment, yet he could sense the question she was putting to him. And finally he said, "I'm a dock laborer, a stevedore. It's rough work, and I guess it gives me a different outlook."

"Not necessarily," she murmured. She pointed to the moonlit river. "We're both seeing the same thing."

"Take a closer look," he said. He gestured toward the splintered pilings of the pier, where scum and garbage were floating. "See that green stuff? That's bilge from the holds of the ships. There's nothing dirtier. If it gets on your skin it crawls right through you. You never get if off you, no matter how hard you scrub. The smell—"

She shuddered. He saw her mouth twisting in a grimace of disgust. She swallowed, pulling in her lower lip.

"Feel sick?" He was grinning at her.

"I'm quite all right," she said.

His eyes were wide and innocent while he told himself to rub it in deep, really let her have it. "I'm only trying to give you the full picture. You come down to see the dirt, I'm showing you the dirt."

"Why do you call it the dirt?"

"That's as good a name as any." He saw the way she was watching him, her eyes intent, and he said, "Don't get too curious, Miss Channing. You're messing around with rough company."

"You're not rough," she said lightly. Then, more seriously, "You remembered my name."

He looked away from her. He didn't say anything.

"You're attracted to me," she said.

He was staring past the windshield, at the dark water of the river. He told himself the best move was to get out of the car and take a walk.

"You're really interested," she said. "Why don't you admit that you're interested?"

There was a strange thick feeling in his throat. He wanted to look at her and he was afraid to look at her.

"Of course," she murmured, "I could be wrong about this. Maybe you just don't go for my type."

"Let it ride."

"I can't."

"That's tough," he said.

"For both of us."

"Not for me."

"You're lying," she said. "You know you're lying."

His fingers gripped the door handle. He begged himself to open the door and get out and walk away.

He heard her saying, "You excite me."

"All right, cut it out."

"But you do," she murmured. "You know you do."

Without looking at her, he knew that she was leaning toward him. He tried to open the door but somehow the handle would not move.

"Look at me," she said.

He looked at her. She was entrancing and he could feel the warmth coming from her body and flowing into him. He told himself he mustn't touch her. His brain pulled frantically at the reins, but she was close and coming closer, sort of floating. Or maybe he was moving toward her, he wasn't sure. The only thing he was sure of was that he was getting dizzy with the nearness of her. And then the reins snapped and there was nothing he could do about it. He had his arms around her and his eyes were closed and he was kissing her.

It was something he'd never felt before, something he'd never known or even imagined. It put him on a cloud going up and away from Vernon Street and the docks and the city, and far away from all the world. It was a feeling of immeasurable delight and it had a flavor that made him terribly thirsty for more and more. But all at once he was able to think. And his brain said, She's just fooling around; all she's doing is getting her kicks in a new way for her.

He pushed her away. He did it roughly and she winced. Then she sat there staring at him and shaking her head slowly. She said, "What happened? What's wrong?"

He couldn't talk.

"Please," she said. "Please tell me what's the matter."

He opened the door and got out of the car. But he couldn't take it past that. He was standing away from the car and wondering why he couldn't move.

"You look frightened," she said. Then, her eyes widening. "You are frightened."

He looked at her. He said very quietly, "Get going."

For a long moment her eyes remained wide. Aside from that, she was quite calm. Finally, with a slight shrug, she started the engine. The MG backed off the pier and drove away.

CHAPTER 6

It was several minutes later and he was on Vernon Street, headed toward home. But as he came closer to the Kerrigan house, he thought of Bella and the battle that would undoubtedly flare up when he got there. She was probably sitting in the parlor waiting for him, and chances were she had some heavy object in her hand, all set to heave it at him the instant he opened the door. Momentarily there was something downright appetizing in the prospect of a clash with Bella. He wanted to hear some noise, and make some himself, and maybe hand her a clout or two. He sure was in the mood for hitting something.

He came to an abrupt stop under a street lamp. No, he told himself, he didn't feel like fighting with Bella. The only thing he felt like hitting right now was his own face. He pulled a pack of cigarettes from his work pants and jabbed one between his tightened lips and struck a match. He leaned against the post of the street lamp, gazing out at the street and taking deep drags of smoke.

A voice called, "Hey, man."

He turned and looked at the window of the wooden shack and saw the long, glimmering earrings, the lacquered black hair, the coffee-and-cream face of Rita Montanez. In the Vernon Street market, which rarely ran as high as three dollars, she alone had the nerve to charge five. She got away with it because she was constructed along the lines that caused men to swallow hard when she passed them on the street. Rita was a mixture of African and Portuguese and she featured the finer physical characteristics of her internationally minded ancestors. Her onyx eyes were long-lashed and she had a finely shaped nose and medium-thick lips. She was in her early thirties and didn't look a day over twenty.

Kerrigan smiled at Rita and walked toward the window. Although he was not a customer, he had a definite affection for her, going back to the days when they were kids playing in the streets.

"Got another smoke?" Rita asked.

He gave her a cigarette and lit it for her.

She winked at him, beckoned with her head, and said, "Wanna come inside?"

He laughed lightly. She laughed with him. They were always going through this routine and taking it just this far and no farther.

"What's new?" she asked. "How's my friend Thomas?"

Kerrigan shrugged. He wasn't affected one way or another by the fact that his father was one of Rita's steady customers. Long ago he'd become accustomed to Tom's dealings with the Vernon professionals.

Rita took an open-mouthed drag at the cigarette. She let the smoke come out slowly, and watched it climbing past her eyes. She said, "I like Thomas. He is much man."

Kerrigan's thoughts were only half focused on what she was saying. He said absently, "You better watch out for Lola."

Rita narrowed her eyes. It was purely technical, an expression of business strategy. "You think Lola knows something?"

He shrugged. "I don't know what she knows. But sooner or later she's gonna pay you a visit. You better be ready to run."

"From her? She's nothing but a lot of fat and a lot of noise." Rita blew smoke away from her face. "Lola don't worry me. No woman worries me." She made a motion toward the back of her head, and her fingers came away holding the tiny black-beetle knob of a five-inch hatpin. "This here's the equalizer," she said. "One jab with this and they know who's boss."

He grinned. "You're a hellcat, Rita."

"Gotta be. This street is no place for softies."

The grin faded. He stared at the splintered wall of the shack. He said, "You got something there."

She studied his eyes. Suddenly she knew what he was thinking. She reached out and touched his arm. "Don't let it get you."

He didn't say anything.

Rita kept her hand on his arm. "I was good friends with your sister."

He blinked. He looked at the painted face of the five-dollar woman.

Rita nodded. "Real good friends," she said. "And I don't make friends easy. Especially women. But it was different with Catherine. She was strictly Grade A."

He stared at Rita. He said, "I didn't know she was friends with you."

"She was friends with everybody." Rita gazed past Kerrigan's head. "I used to see her giving candy to the kids in the street. Giving pennies to the bums and the cripples. Always giving."

His voice was thick. "She sure got paid back nice."

"Don't think about that."

For some moments he didn't speak. And then very low in his throat, "It was my fault."

She looked at him. She frowned.

He said, "I knew she didn't belong here. I should have taken her away."

"Where?"

"Anywhere," he said. "Just to get her away from this mess. This goddamn street."

"You don't like the street?"

"Look at it." He pointed to the rutted paving, the choked gutter, the littered doorsteps. "What's there to like?"

"She liked it," Rita said.

"She had no choice. She lived here all her life and she never knew anything better."

"But she liked it. She was happy here. That's what you gotta remember."

"I can only remember one thing: I could have taken her out of this fouled-up rut and I didn't do it."

"Quit blaming yourself," Rita said.

"There's no one else to blame."

"Yes, there is. But there's no way to point at him, you don't know his name. Maybe you'll never know. After all, it happened almost a year ago. Best thing for you to do is forget about it."

He wanted to say something, to disagree with Rita's viewpoint, but as he searched for a way it was like groping in a dark closet that had no walls. He shook his head slowly, futilely, and finally he murmured, "Goodnight, Rita," and walked away.

At the corner of Fourth and Vernon he took out his pocket watch. The hands pointed to twenty past three. He had to be up very early and it hardly paid to go home and get in bed. And now the prospect of a battle with Bella was not at all appetizing. He winced at the thought that she'd still be sitting up, preparing to greet him with a flood of curses. Suddenly he was thinking of the railway ticket office, the bus depot, the freighters docked at the piers. But that had nothing to do with Bella. He just felt like taking off, that was all. He just wanted a long trip that would carry him far away from Vernon Street.

Skip it, he told himself. Think about it later.

He shrugged. But it was more than a casual effort. His shoulders felt strangely heavy. And then trying to shake off the weighted feeling, he began to walk fast. But suddenly he came to an abrupt halt. He turned his head slowly and looked at the dark alley, where moonlight fell on a broken bottle, a crushed tin can, and the dried bloodstains of his sister.

He moved toward the alley. Then he was in the alley, looking down at the bloodstains. He wondered why his eyes felt cold. Quit it, he told himself. Get out of here. Go home. But he stood there looking down at the crimson stains on the rutted paving. A minute passed, another minute, and then all at once he had the feeling that someone was watching him.

He turned very slowly. He saw the carrot-colored hair and thick neck and sloping shoulders of Mooney. The sign painter had his head slanted and his arms folded and seemed to be appraising Kerrigan as though lining him up for a charcoal sketch.

Kerrigan smiled uncertainly. "I didn't know you were there."

"Just happened to see you," Mooney said. He shifted his position, leaning against the wall of the shack at the edge of the alley. His hair was damp and shiny.

"Enjoy your swim? Cool you off any?" Kerrigan asked.

Mooney had a look of grumbling displeasure. "That goddamn river. Cooled me off, hell. Only thing it did, it almost drowned me."

Kerrigan grinned. "Was Nick there to see it?"

Mooney nodded. He said offhandedly, "Reached me just in time. I went down twice before he dived in."

Kerrigan was still grinning. "Where's Nick now?"

"Went home. That's what I oughta do." He shrugged again. Then he looked at Kerrigan and said quietly, "Making progress?"

"What?" Kerrigan said. "What are you talking about?"

"This situation here," Mooney murmured. He was looking down at the bloodstains. "I've seen you in this alley more times than I can count. Of course, it ain't none of my business—"

"All right, let's drop it."

"You won't drop it."

"I'm dropping it now. It's a dead issue."

"The hell it is. You'll come here again. You'll keep coming here."

"If I do, I'm a damn fool," Kerrigan said.

"I wouldn't say that." Mooney spoke very quietly, almost in a whisper. "I've never had you checked off as a damn fool."

For a long moment they stood there looking at each other. Then Mooney said, "You come here to investigate."

"There's nothing to investigate," Kerrigan said. But while he said it, he was making a careful study of Mooney's face, especially the eyes. He went on, trying to speak casually. "She did away with herself. There's no question about that. She picked up a rusty blade and cut her throat and then she laid down to die. So the point is, she did it with her own hands. I'm not trying to take it past that."

"It goes a long way past that," Mooney said. "She did it because she was ruined and she couldn't stand the pain or the grief or whatever it was. There's never been any secret about that. You weren't here when it happened, but there was a big commotion and the entire neighborhood was looking for the man who did it. You see, everybody liked her. I liked her very much."

"You did?"

"Yes," Mooney said. "Very much."

"I didn't know you were acquainted with her."

"Don't look at me like that," Mooney said.

"What's the matter?" Kerrigan said gently.

"I don't like the way you're looking at me." Mooney's face was expressionless. "Don't jockey with me. I'm talking straight."

"I hope so," Kerrigan said. "How well were you acquainted? I never saw you talking to her."

"We talked many times," Mooney said. "Someone told her I used to paint pictures. She liked to talk about painting. She wanted to learn about it. One time I showed her some of my water colors."

"Where? In your room?"

"Sure."

Kerrigan looked at Mooney's thick neck. He said, "She wouldn't go into a man's room."

"She would if she trusted the man."

"How do you know she trusted you?"

"She told me," Mooney said.

"Can you prove it?"

"Prove what?"

"That you're on the level."

Mooney frowned slightly. "I'm sorry I started this," he said to himself. Then, gazing directly at Kerrigan, "You're suspicious of everybody, aren't you?"

"Not exactly," Kerrigan said. "I'm just doing a lot of thinking, that's all."

"Yes, I can see that." Mooney was nodding slowly. "You're doing a hell of a lot of thinking."

Kerrigan took a slow deep breath. Then he said very quietly, "I'd like you and me to take a little walk."

"Where?"

"To your room."

"What for?" Mooney asked. "What's in my room?"

"The water-color paintings," Kerrigan said. He smiled dimly and added, "Or maybe there's no paintings at all. Maybe there's just a bed. I'd like to have a look and make sure."

Mooney's face was blank. "You're checking on me?"

"Sure," Kerrigan said, and he widened the smile.

For some moments Mooney didn't move. Finally he shrugged and backed out of the alley and Kerrigan moved up beside him. They walked down Vernon Street toward Third. Near the corner of Third and Vernon they turned down another alley. It was very narrow and there were no lights in the windows of the wooden shacks. Mooney was walking slowly and Kerrigan followed him and watched him very carefully. Mooney's shoulders were sort of hunched, his arms bent just a little and held away from his sides, and he seemed to be bracing himself for something.

"You there?" Mooney asked.

"Right behind you."

Mooney slowed to a stop. He started to turn his head.

"Keep moving," Kerrigan said.

"Listen, Bill—"

"No," Kerrigan cut in. "You can't stall now. You're taking me to your room."

"I only want to say—"

"You'll say it later. Keep moving."

Mooney walked on. Kerrigan followed him and they went halfway down the alley and arrived at a two-story shack that had no doorstep and no glass in the front windows. Mooney went up to the door and then he stopped again and started to move his head to get a look at Kerrigan.

"Inside," Kerrigan said.

"Bill, you've known me all your life."

"I wonder," Kerrigan murmured. Then, through his teeth, "Go on, get inside. Get the hell inside."

Mooney opened the door. They came into a room where a lot of people were sleeping. There weren't enough beds and the floor was a jumble of sleeping grownups and children. Kerrigan stayed close behind Mooney, treading carefully to avoid stepping on the sleepers on the floor. They made their way across the room and went into another room where there were more sleepers. For an instant Kerrigan forgot about Mooney and he was wondering how many families lived in this dump. Goddamn them, he thought, they don't hafta live like this. At least they can keep the place clean. But then his mind aimed again at Mooney and he saw the sign painter turning toward the stairway. And he thought, Be careful now, it might happen when we're halfway up the stairs.

But nothing happened. Mooney didn't even look back. They came up on the second floor and went down a very narrow hall. The ceiling was low and there wasn't much air. It seemed there was hardly any air at all.

He followed Mooney into a room. It was a tiny room and there was no furniture. The only thing he saw was a mattress on the floor. But then Mooney switched on the light, and other objects came into view.

There was a large vase, almost four feet high. It was some kind of glazed stone and was cracked in many places and looked very old. Kerrigan looked to see what was in it and he saw it was filled with cigarette stubs and ashes. Next to the vase there was a stack of large rough-surfaced paper used for water-color paintings. And then he saw the jars of paint, the little tubes, and the brushes. Paint brushes of various sizes were scattered all over the room. He figured there must be at least a hundred brushes in here. He came closer to the stack of papers and lifted the edges and saw that some of the sheets hadn't been used. But the others were all water-color landscapes and still lifes and a few portraits. And that was what he had come here to see. It was the tangible proof that Mooney hadn't been lying.

"Well," he said quietly, "you got the paintings here, all right."

He waited for a reply. There was no reply. He turned slowly to look at Mooney, who stood facing the wall on the other side of the room. Then there was no sound in the room, not even the sound of breathing.

They were both looking at the wall and what was on the wall.

It was a rather large water color on thick board paper. It was the only painting on any of the walls. The dominant color was the yellow-gray background for the greenish-gray of her face and the cocoa-gray-yellow of her hair. It was just the head and neck and shoulders against the background. The head was slightly lowered and there wasn't much expression on the face and it was merely the portrait of a very thin girl with long hair, not much to look at, really. But she was alive there on the wall. She seemed to be living and breathing and fully conscious of what she was and who she was. She was Catherine Kerrigan.

"I didn't want you to see it," Mooney said. "I tried to tell you."

Kerrigan was moving backward. He kept moving backward until he bumped into the large vase. He reached back and gripped the edge of the vase. His fingers merged with the glazed stone and then his arms felt like stone and he wondered if his entire body were turning to stone. He was looking at his sister and telling himself she couldn't be dead.

He heard Mooney saying, "Damn it, I tried to tell you. I didn't want you to come here."

"It's all right," he said. But the words meant nothing.

He looked at her up there on the wall and without sound said, Catherine, Catherine.

And then without seeing Mooney's face, he was hit by something coming out of Mooney's eyes. He looked at Mooney and knew the way it was, the way it must have been for a long time, and the way it would always be. The knowledge of it came to him very slowly, going into him very deep and pushing aside all the shock and astonishment, causing him to understand fully that Mooney had worshiped her and would go on worshiping her.

For some moments he stood looking at Mooney and they were having a silent conversation. They were

talking about her, telling each other what a special item
she'd been, and all the kindness and sweetness of her
nature, the gentle manner and the sincerity. In the quiet
of the room she gazed down at them and it seemed she
joined them in their soundless discussion, saying, Don't
give me such a build-up. I didn't really amount to much,
just another Vernon girl with very little brains and no
looks at all.

Mooney spoke aloud. "She was quality. The real
quality."

Suddenly Kerrigan felt very tired. He looked around
for a place to sit. Finally he sat down on the mattress on
the floor. He folded his hands around his bent knees and
lowered his head and his eyes were half closed.

He heard Mooney saying, "She never knew how I felt
about her. I'm not sure if I can tell it to you now."

"I think I know already."

"No, you don't," Mooney said. "She was your sister,
and it's an entirely different feeling. You never had to
fight against something inside, something that said you
were male and she was female. I wanted her so much
that I used to steal from drugstores to poison myself so
I'd get an upset stomach and have the cramps to think
about."

Kerrigan looked at him.

"Why didn't you let her know?"

"I couldn't. She'd have felt sorry for me. She might
have done something that she didn't want to do. Just to
make things easier for me. It would have been an act of
charity. You see, if I thought she went for me, I'd have
asked her to marry me."

"You should have told her."

Mooney sighed slowly. He looked at the floor. He said,

"She was clean. And I'm a dirty man. It's the kind of dirt that don't wash off. It's in too deep. Too many memories of dirty places and dirty women."

"You're not so dirty. And I think you should have told her."

"Well maybe I wasn't man enough." Mooney turned and looked up at the picture on the wall.

Kerrigan looked at Mooney and felt very sorry for him and couldn't say anything.

"Not man enough," Mooney said. "Just a specialist in the art of wasting time and lousing things up. There was a time the critics had me ranked with the important names in water color. They said I'd soon be pushing Marin for the number-one spot on the list. Today I'm pushing the sale of window signs for butcher stores and tailor shops. My weekly income, according to latest reports, is anywhere from twelve to fifteen dollars. If the Treasury Department is interested, the current bankroll is a dollar and sixty-seven cents."

Mooney was telling it to the dead girl, speaking in a conversational tone, as though he thought she could actually hear what he was saying.

"Comes a time," he told the painted face on the wall, "when the battery runs down, the stamina gives out, and a man just don't care any more. That happened long ago with this fine citizen. Not a damn thing I could have done for you, except lean on your shoulder and weigh you down. I'm a great leaner, one of the finest. I have a remarkable talent for making people tired."

Kerrigan figured it was time for him to say something. "You have a pretty fair talent for painting pictures." He gazed at the portrait on the wall.

"Thank you," Mooney said quietly and formally, as

though he were addressing an art critic. Then his tone became technical. "There was no live model. This work was painted from memory. There were more than thirty preliminary sketches. The portrait took three months to complete, and this is the first time it's been exhibited."

Kerrigan nodded, although he was scarcely listening. He went on looking at the painted face that was framed there on the wall and gradually it became a living face as the gears of time shifted into reverse, taking him backward five years to a summer night when he stood with Catherine on the corner of Second and Vernon. He'd been walking up Second Street and he'd seen her leaning against the lamppost on the corner. Coming closer, he'd noticed that she was breathing heavily, as though she'd been running. He said, "What's wrong?" and for some moments she didn't answer, and then she smiled and shrugged and said, "It's really nothing." But he knew the smile was forced, and the shrug was an effort to hide something.

He put his hands on Catherine's shoulders. He said quietly, "Come on, tell me."

She tried to hold the smile, tried to shrug again. But somehow she couldn't manage it. Her lips quivered. Her pale face became paler. All at once she gripped his arms, as though to keep herself from falling, and she said, "I'm so glad you're here."

"Catherine." His voice was gentle. "Tell me what happened."

She hesitated. Then, whatever the issue was, she made an attempt to evade it. She said, "You look so tired and worn out. Work hard today?"

"Overtime," he replied. "They were short of men." In the glow of the street lamp he saw the delicate line of her features, the fragility of her body. She always wore low-heeled shoes and loose-waisted schoolgirl dresses and looked much younger than eighteen. The dress was cotton, plain drab gray, and it needed sewing here and there. But it was clean. She wouldn't wear anything that wasn't clean.

She was smiling again and saying, "You really look knocked out. Let's go somewhere and sit down."

She was always saying, "Let's go somewhere," as if there were anywhere to go except the candy store, which had a small fountain and a few battered stools.

"Come on," she said. "I'll treat you to a soda."

She took his hand. He sensed she was anxious to get off the corner. They walked two blocks to the little candy store and went in and sat down at the fountain. She asked him what he wanted and he said, "Orange," and she put a dime on the counter and ordered two bottles of orange pop.

He took a few long gulps and his bottle was empty. She sipped hers from a straw. He watched her as she sat there taking tiny sips and enjoying the flavor of the soda. There was a look of pleasure on her face and he thought, It takes so little to please her.

Suddenly he got off the stool and went to the magazine rack. She liked movie magazines and he stood there checking them to see if there was one that she hadn't read yet. He was reaching for a magazine when the door opened and three young men came into the candy store. They sort of barged in, and he turned and looked at them. They were wearing torn shirts and ragged trousers and battered shoes. It was hard to tell which one of them was the ugliest, which face was most misshapen.

The three of them were winking at each other as they moved toward Catherine. She was still sipping the soda and hadn't yet seen them. Kerrigan was waiting to see what they'd do. He saw the shortest one, who looked like a middleweight, slide onto the seat next to Catherine. The middleweight grinned at her and said, "Well, whaddya know? We meet again."

Catherine was trembling slightly. Kerrigan had a fairly adequate notion as to why she'd been out of breath when he'd met her on the corner.

The middleweight went on grinning at her. The other two were snickering. One of them was scar-faced and the other featured a yellowish complexion and crooked buck teeth that prevented him from closing his mouth. Scarface sat down so that Catherine was hemmed in between him and the middleweight. Then Scarface said something in low tones that Kerrigan couldn't hear, and Catherine winced. She turned her head to see Kerrigan standing there at the magazine rack. He gave her a re-assuring nod, as though to say, Don't worry, I'm still here. I just want to see how far they'll take it.

The middleweight widened the grin. It became a grimace as he said to Catherine, "Why'd you run away?"

Catherine didn't answer. The aged candy-store proprietor was standing behind the counter and scowling at the three young men and saying, "Well? Well?"

"Well what?" Scarface said.

"This is a store. Whatcha wanna buy?"

"We ain't in no hurry," the middleweight said. He turned to Catherine. "I like to take my time. It makes things more interesting." He edged closer to her.

"Please go away," Catherine said.

The proprietor was pointing to a sign on the wall

behind the counter. "You read English?" he demanded of the three young men. "It says, 'No Loafing.' "

"We're not loafing," the middleweight said mildly. "We're here to keep a date, that's all."

Catherine started to get up from the stool. But she was crowded from all sides and they wouldn't give her room. Kerrigan didn't move. He told himself he would wait until one of them put a hand on her.

The proprietor took another deep breath. "This is a store," he repeated. "If you're not here to buy something, get out."

"All right, Pop." The middleweight reached into his pocket and took out a dollar bill. "Three root-beer floats." He made a casual reach for the bottle in Catherine's trembling hand. He took the bottle away from her and said to the proprietor, "Make it four."

Catherine looked at the middleweight. She wasn't trembling now. There was just the slightest trace of a smile on her lips. It was a kind smile, something pitying in it. She said very softly, "I'm sorry I ran away from you and your friends. But you were talking sort of rough, and then when you came toward me—"

"I wasn't gonna hurt ya," the middleweight said. He was frowning just a little: he seemed uncertain of what to say next. He aimed the frown at Scarface and Bucktooth, as though blaming them for something. Catherine went on smiling at the middleweight. Gradually his frown faded. "Damn. I shoulda known how it was from the way you walked. You didn't swing it like them teasers do."

Catherine grinned. She looked down at her skinny body. She gave a little shrug and said, "I got nothing to swing."

The middleweight laughed, and the other two joined in. Kerrigan told himself to relax. It was all right now. He saw Bucktooth sitting down beside Scarface and the proprietor placing four root-beer floats on the counter and he heard the middleweight saying, "Hey, look, my name is Mickey. And that's Pete. And that's Wally."

"I'm Catherine," she said. She turned and beckoned to Kerrigan, and he came forward. "This is Bill," she said. "My brother."

"Hi," the middleweight said. He told the proprietor to mix another root-beer float.

Kerrigan wasn't thirsty now, but he decided to drink the float anyway. He thanked the middleweight and saw the pleased smile on Catherine's face. She was happy because everyone was friendly.

He sipped the root-beer float and listened to the soft voice of Catherine as she chatted with the three young hoodlums. Her voice was like a soothing touch. He looked at the face of his sister and saw the gentle radiance in her eyes.

Then time shifted gears again and it was now, it was Mooney's room again. He was sitting there on the mattress on the floor and staring up at the portrait on the wall.

"You look knocked out," Mooney said. "Why don't you roll over and go to sleep?"

He gazed dully at Mooney. "Gotta be up early. There's no alarm clock."

"That's all right. I'll wake you. Got a watch?"

Kerrigan was already prone on the mattress and his eyes were closed as he took out the pocket watch and handed it to Mooney. "Get me up at six-thirty," he whispered, and while sleep closed in on his brain he wondered what Mooney would be doing awake at that time. But before he could put the question into words, he was asleep.

CHAPTER 7

At ten in the morning the sun was like a big muzzle shooting liquid fire onto the river. Near the docks the big ships glimmered in the sticky heat. On the piers the stevedores were stripped bare to the waist, and some of them had rags tied around their foreheads to keep the perspiration from running into their eyes.

Alongside Pier 17 there was a freighter that had just come in from the West Indies with a cargo of pineapples, and the dock foremen were feverishly bawling orders, spurring the stevedores to work faster. There were some wholesale fruit merchants scurrying around, screaming that pineapples were rotting on the deck, melting away in the heat, while these goddamn loafers took their time and carried the crates as though they had lead in their pants.

Kerrigan and two other workers were struggling with a six-hundred-pound crate when a little man wearing a straw hat came up and shrieked, "Lift it! For God's sake, lift it!"

They were trying to lift the crate onto a wheeled platform. But on this side of the pier there was a traffic problem. They were surrounded by a jam-up of crates and bales and huge boxes and they had insufficient space to get leverage.

Stooped over, with the crate leaning against their backs, the two stevedores were panting and grimacing while Kerrigan knelt on the planks, his hands under the edge of the crate, trying to coax it onto the platform.

"You morons!" the little man screeched. "That ain't the way to do it."

The edge of the crate came onto the platform. The wheels of the platform moved just a little and the crate slipped off. Kerrigan's hands were under the crate and he pulled them away just in time.

"I told you," the little man yelled. "You see?"

One of the stevedores looked at the little man. Then he looked at Kerrigan and said, "All right, Bill. Let's try it again."

The other stevedore was arching his back and rubbing his spine and saying, "We need more room here."

The little man shouted, "You need more brains, that's what you need."

Kerrigan wiped sweat from his face. He took his position at the side of the crate, pushed a smaller box against the platform to keep it from rolling, and said to the stevedores, "Ready now?"

"All set."

"Heave," Kerrigan grunted, and the men braced their backs under the weight of the crate, while Kerrigan strained to work it onto the platform. Again he managed to lift it over the edge, but just then a sliver of rusty metal went stabbing into his fingernail and he lost his hold on the crate. "Goddamnit," he muttered as the crate fell off the platform and slammed onto the planks of the pier. He stood up and put the injured finger in his mouth and sucked at the blood.

"Go in deep?" one of the stevedores said.

"It's all right." Kerrigan winced and took his finger

out of his mouth and looked at the torn cuticle. He said,
"I guess it's all right."

"It don't look good, Bill. You better have it bandaged."

"The hell with it," Kerrigan said.

The little man was hopping up and down and shouting, "What are you standing around for? What about the
pineapples? Look at the pineapples. They're rotting away
in the sun." He beckoned to a dock foreman on the other
side of the pier. "Hey, Ruttman. Come here, I want you
to see this."

The dock foreman made his way through a gap in the
pile-up of pineapple crates. He was a very big man in his
late thirties. His head was partially bald and he had a
flattened nose and thick scarred lips and a lot of chin
and jaw. His arms were tattoed from wrist to shoulder
and the hair on his chest was like a screen of foliage in
front of the large tattoo, the purple-brown-black head of
an African water buffalo.

As Ruttman approached, the little man continued to
hop up and down, yelling, "What kind of men you got
working here? Take a look at this situation."

"Easy, Johnny, easy." Ruttman had a deep, furry voice.
He came up to the crate, glanced at the wheeled plat-
form, and then looked at the three stevedores. He said,
"What goes on here?"

"We just can't handle it," one of them said. "We ain't
got enough space to work in."

"You're a liar," the little man shrieked. "There's plenty
of space. You're just goofing, that's all, you're trying to
kill time."

Ruttman told the little man to go away. The little man
started to yelp, claiming that he had a lot of money in-
vested in these pineapples and he'd be damned if he was

going to let them get spoiled. Ruttman said the pine-apples wouldn't get spoiled and it would help matters if the little man went away. The little man folded his arms and shouted he was going to stay right here. Ruttman sighed wearily and took a slow step toward the little man. The little man scampered away.

The three stevedores moved toward the crate and Ruttman shook his head, waving them back and saying, "This ain't no good. We gotta do it another way." He looked at Kerrigan. "Bring me a chain and a crowbar."

Kerrigan turned and walked down along the length of the pier, wiping sweat from his face. In the tool shed he found a roll of adhesive tape, and he cut off a strip and slipped it around his torn finger. He came out of the shed carrying the heavy chain and the crowbar. He took a few steps and stopped short and the crowbar fell out of his hand, the chain slipped away from his fingers. He stood motionless, staring at Loretta Channing.

She was sitting at the wheel of the MG. The car was parked on the pier. A few men wearing Panama hats and tropical-weave suits were leaning against the car and it was evident she'd got special permission to come onto the pier.

As Kerrigan stood there, unable to breathe, Loretta waved to him. He could feel the heavy awkwardness of the moment as the men in Panama hats turned to look at him, their faces showing vaguely puzzled smiles.

He told himself to pick up the chain and crowbar and get out of here. But as he reached down, he stiffened again. He was staring at an object in Loretta's hands. It was a small camera. She had it focused on him.

He straightened, breathing air that seemed to burn. His arms were away from his sides, his hands were clenched, and he didn't realize he was showing his teeth.

The camera made a clicking sound. It was a very small noise, but in his brain it was amplified. It cracked like a lash hitting him in the face.

He moved toward the MG. He walked very slowly. His head jutted like an aimed weapon. A fruit clerk wearing an apron came into his path and he pushed the man aside, not hearing the whine of protest. The men in Panama hats were moving uneasily as they detected the menace in his approach. Instinctively they got out of his way. But Loretta didn't move. Loretta sat there at the wheel, smiling at him, waiting for him, the camera held loosely in her hand.

He came up to the door of the MG and pointed to the camera and said, "Give it to me."

Loretta widened her eyes in mock surprise. "You want it for a gift?"

"All I want is the film."

The mockery remained on her face. "What will you do with it?"

"I'd like to shove it down your throat."

The men in Panama hats were swallowing hard and looking at each other. One of them braced himself and tapped Kerrigan on the shoulder and murmured, "No need to take offense, fellow. All the lady did was take your picture."

"You keep out of it," Kerrigan said.

The man said, "Now look here, I'm one of the owners of this pier."

Ignoring the man, Kerrigan reached out toward the camera. But Loretta was faster. She opened the panel of the glove compartment, slid the camera in, and closed the panel.

Kerrigan gripped the door, leaned across the steering wheel, and moved his hand toward the glove compartment. The pier owner grabbed his arm and said, "Just a moment here. Just a moment."

In the next instant the Panama hat was falling off the pier owner's head. He was shoved backward, with Kerrigan's flat hand covering his face. He tripped over a loose plank and sat down very hard and stared up at Kerrigan with his mouth opened wide.

Loretta hadn't moved. She was smiling at Kerrigan and saying, "I can't understand why you're so upset. All I did was take your picture."

His voice was low and even but it whipped at her. "You want it for a souvenir. You'll show it to your uptown friends. Picture of a man, stripped almost naked, like something on exhibit in a cage."

Again he reached for the glove compartment. Loretta sat there quietly, making no move to stop him as his finger found the chromium button. He pressed the button, the panel swung open, and he groped for the camera. His hand closed on it and he pulled it out and at that moment he felt the iron pressure coming down on his arm, gripping him above the elbow and causing him to blink.

He turned his head and saw the face of Ruttman.

"Easy, bud," the dock foreman murmured. "Easy now."

"Let go." He tried to jerk his arm away, but Ruttman held him there.

The pier owner, still hatless, had come forward and was saying to Ruttman, "Throw this man off the dock. Give him his pay and get him out of here."

"Yes, sir," Ruttman said. He took a deep breath that was like a sigh. "All right, bud. Let's go."

Kerrigan didn't move. He was looking at the faces of the men with the Panama hats. They were smiling at him; they felt safe now. They saw him taken in charge by a larger man, a stronger man, a man who was obviously capable of handling him.

"I said let's go." Ruttman's tone was louder.

But he didn't hear it. He was staring at the other faces, the faces of the stevedores who'd left the crates and were moving in to see what would happen. Ruttman was the undisputed boss of Pier 17 and there were scores of dock-wallopers who'd tried their best to disprove it, only to get their teeth knocked out, their noses caved in, their jaws broken. All along the docks of Wharf Street the opinion was unanimous: It never paid to trifle with Ruttman.

Kerrigan looked at the face of Ruttman and saw the strength, the quiet confidence, saw the warning that was almost friendly. Ruttman's eyes seemed to be saying, Don't force me into it, I really don't want to hurt you.

And then, as caution was mixed with the reasonable knowledge that he had no complaint against Ruttman, he turned his head, a gesture of submittal. In that instant he saw Loretta smiling at him, a mocking smile.

He let the camera fall way from his fingers, and the back of his hand cracked across her mouth.

It was a hard blow and it sent her head twisting all the way to the side. But he didn't have time to see what damage he had done, because Ruttman was already hitting him.

Ruttman was smashing him with a straight right that caught him under the eye. He fell back with his arms wide, his feet off the ground. He collided with a crate, bounced away, started to fall, made up his mind he wouldn't fall, and lunged at Ruttman with his fists flailing.

He found Ruttman's head with his right hand, staggered Ruttman with another blow to the temple, then came in close and ripped both hands to the body. He heard Ruttman grunting and again he punched to the body, and Ruttman started to double up, falling forward, trying to clinch.

Kerrigan stepped back and hooked a short left to Ruttman's jaw, followed it with another left to the side of the head, stepping back again and chopping with the right and missing, and then taking a terrible, thundering blow from Ruttman's right hand. It was a round-house smash, a punch that started wide, came in short, exploded on his jaw, and knocked him down.

"That winds it up," someone said.

Kerrigan's eyes were closed and he was flat on his back. There was no pain, only the feeling of wanting to stay here and keep sinking into the darkness.

But then he heard a voice saying, "Finished?"

He opened his eyes and looked up and saw Ruttman. He grinned and said, "Not yet."

Ruttman sighed reluctantly and stepped back, giving him a chance to get up. He got up slowly, now feeling the pain, the grogginess, and it was as though his jaw were bolted to his skull and a wrench were tightening the bolt.

He saw Ruttman walking in to measure him, the right hand taking aim. In Ruttman's eyes there was no satisfaction. Ruttman came in close, feinted with the left, and threw the right.

Kerrigan moved his head, got away from the big fist, blocked a left that tried to find his ribs, blocked the right

coming again toward his jaw, then side-stepped going
away from another right. Ruttman grunted, lunged,
missed with both hands, lunged again, and missed again
as Kerrigan crouched going backward, weaving and
dodging, ducking and coming up and then moving away
from where Ruttman wanted him to be.

Ruttman's expression had changed. Now his eyes
showed impatience. He took a deep breath and charged
at Kerrigan, putting everything he had in an overhand
right that whizzed toward Kerrigan's head. The fist hit
empty air and nothing else. Ruttman lost his balance
and stumbled and fell to one knee.

Someone laughed.

Ruttman came up fast. He rushed again, his left arm
swinging hard. Kerrigan went inside the hook, shot a
short right to Ruttman's belly, used the right again,
ripping it to the ribs. Ruttman lowered his hands to
protect his midsection, and Kerrigan took a backward
step, took aim, and hauled off and smashed a straight
right hand to the chin.

He saw Ruttman staggering sideways, the thick arms
flailing. The dock foreman struggled to keep his balance,
managed to hold on and stay on his feet, moving
unsteadily, eyes dull, then bracing himself and coming
in again.

Kerrigan was ready. He jabbed with his left, jabbed
again and again finding Ruttman's nose and mouth.
Then another vicious jab that had all his strength behind
it, his fist twisting as it landed against Ruttman's brow.
He saw the flaring red streak above Ruttman's eye, and
he sent another left to the same place, that widened the
cut.

The dock workers were silent, staring in disbelief as

they saw Ruttman taking it and falling backward and still taking it. They were watching the downfall of a man they believed to be invincible. And they didn't like it.

Kerrigan put another left against Ruttman's bad eye. Ruttman let out a groan of pain, tried to cover up, and Kerrigan, working very fast now, hooked a left to the head, hooked again to the body, chopped with the right and brought more blood and a couple of teeth from Ruttman's mouth.

Someone yelled, "Come on, Ruttman! Don't take it. Go after him."

"Get him, Ruttman!"

"Knock his brains out!"

As the stevedores shouted encouragement to Ruttman, it was like a heavy weight falling on Kerrigan's chest. Suddenly he realized he was fighting a man he had no right to fight. He was defeating the man and he hated the idea.

Because the adversary was not Ruttman. The true enemy was sitting there at the wheel of the parked car, her golden hair glimmering, her eyes taunting him.

It was as though she were saying, You're afraid of me.

He could hear the grinding of his teeth as he realized it was true. He had the feeling of facing a high fence, much too high for him to climb. The fists of Ruttman were coming toward him but it wasn't important, he didn't care. He scarcely felt the knuckles that bashed his face. It wasn't a fight any longer, it was just a mess, a loused-up comedy without any laughs.

Something crashed against his mouth. He tasted blood, but he wasn't conscious of the taste, or the grinding pain.

He was thinking, You can't handle her, you know you can't.

A big fist hit him on the side of the head, sent him falling back. He saw Ruttman moving in for the follow-up, saw Ruttman's arms coming in like pistons. But it didn't matter. He didn't even bother to lift his hands.

His head jerked to the side as Ruttman's right hand caught him on the jaw. Ruttman hit him in the mid-section with a short ripping left that caused him to double up, then straightened him with a long left, then another right to the jaw, setting him up now, gauging him, sort of propping him there, and then winding it up and sending it in, a package of thunder that became a flashing, blinding streak of light going up from his chin to his brain. He sailed back and went down like a falling plank and rolled over on his face.

The onlookers stood motionless for several moments. Then a few stevedores moved forward to join Ruttman, who was bending over Kerrigan and muttering, "He's out. He's out cold."

"Is he breathing?"

"He's all right," Ruttman said.

They turned Kerrigan over so that he rested on his back. For a few seconds they were silent, just staring at his face.

His eyes were closed, but the men weren't looking at his eyes. They were watching his mouth.

"He's smiling," one of them said. "Look at this crazy bastard. What's he got to smile about?"

Kerrigan was deep in the soothing darkness and far away from everything, yet his blacked-out brain was speaking to him, smiling and saying derisively, You damn fool.

CHAPTER 8

They lifted Kerrigan and carried him into the pier office and put him on a battered leather sofa in the dusty back room that was used for infirmary purposes. They splashed water in his face and worked some whisky down his throat, and within a few minutes he was sitting up and accepting a cigarette from Ruttman. He took a long drag and smiled amiably at the dock foreman.

Ruttman smiled back. "Hurt much?" Kerrigan shrugged.

The other stevedores were slowly leaving the office. Ruttman waited until all of them were gone and then he said, "You gave me a damn nice tussle. For a while there you had me going. But all of a sudden you quit cold. Why?"

Kerrigan shrugged again. "Ran out of gas."

"No, you didn't. You were doing fine." Ruttman's eyes narrowed. "Come on, tell me why you quit."

"I just lost interest. I got bored."

Ruttman sighed. "Guess I'll have to let it ride." And then, deciding on a final try, "If you'll open up, maybe I can help you."

"Who needs help?"

"You do," Ruttman said. "For one thing, you're out of a job."

Kerrigan tried to take it casually, but he felt the bite of genuine panic as he thought of the family's financial condition. His weekly pay check was the only money coming into the house these days. Of course, there were

Bella's three nights a week as a hat-check girl, but she had the gambling habit, mostly horses, and she was always in the red. So here he was with five mouths to feed and no job and the picture was definitely unfunny.

He made an effort to cheer himself up. "This ain't the only pier on the river. I'll go see Ferraco on Nineteen. He's always got a shortage."

"No," Ruttman said. "He won't hire you. None of them'll hire you."

"Why not?" he asked, but he already knew the answer.

"You're blackballed," Ruttman said. "It's going down the line already."

Kerrigan stared down at the uncarpeted floor. He took another drag at the cigarette and it tasted sour.

He heard Ruttman saying, "I'd like to go to bat, but you won't give me anything to work on."

He went on staring at the floor. "The hell with it."

Ruttman let out a huge sigh. "I guess it ain't no use," he said aloud to himself. Then, looking at Kerrigan, "Better stay here and rest a while. When you come out, I'll have your pay check ready."

The dock foreman walked out of the room. Kerrigan sat there on the edge of the sofa, feeling the dizziness coming again, starting to feel the full hurt of the big fists that had rammed his ribs and his belly and his face. Very slowly he pulled his legs onto the sofa and lay back. He closed his eyes and told himself to fade away for an hour or so.

Just then he heard a footstep, the rustle of a dress. He opened his eyes and saw Loretta Channing looking down at him.

She stood there at the side of the sofa, her hands holding the camera. She wasn't aiming it, and he saw that her fingers were manipulating a lever and getting the camera open and taking out a small roll of film.

Her face was expressionless as she extended her hand to offer him the film.

He grinned wryly and shook his head.

"Take it," she said.

"What'll I do with it?"

"Whatever you wish. You said you'd like to shove it down my throat."

He went on grinning. "Did I really say that?"

She nodded. Then she stepped back a little, studying him. Her eyebrows were lifted slightly, as though she was seeing something she hadn't expected to see. He knew she'd anticipated another bitter outburst from him, another display of uncontrollable rage.

He lowered his legs over the side of the sofa, then leaned back, comfortably relaxed. He watched her as she walked across the room and dropped the roll of film into a waste basket. Then she turned and looked at him and she was waiting for him to say something.

He saw the bruise on her lip, and he winced.

"I'm sorry I hit you," he said. Then, with the feeling that he had to say more, he added, "I didn't mean to do it. Just lost my head for a second." He stood up and moved toward the window that looked out upon the sun-drenched river. His voice was very low, not much more than a husky whisper. "I'm really very sorry."

It was quiet for a few moments. Then he heard her say, "Please don't apologize. I'm glad you did it."

He turned and looked at her.

"Yes," she said, "I know I deserved it. I shouldn't have come out there on the pier, and I certainly had no right to snap your picture."

"Why did you do it?"

She opened her mouth to answer. Then she changed her mind and her lips shut tightly. He saw her face go red. She blinked a few times, then looked past him and said, "Whatever my reasons were, it was inexcusable, and I'm very much ashamed of myself." With an effort she gazed directly at his face. "I hope you'll forgive me."

For some strange reason he wasn't able to meet her eyes. He looked at the floor and swallowed hard. "It's all right," he said gruffly. "Let's forget it."

"I can't. I want you to know how badly I feel about this. I've caused you a lot of trouble. You took a bad beating out there on the dock. And now they tell me you've been fired."

He rubbed the back of his neck. "Well, that's the way it goes. I was looking for grief, so they gave it to me."

"But it's all my fault," she said. And then, in a lower tone, "Won't you let me make it up to you?"

He looked at her. "How?"

"I know one of the pier owners. I'll tell him it wasn't your fault. Maybe he'll let you keep your job."

His eyes hardened, and he could feel the cold anger coming. But as he stood there and looked at her, his gaze gradually narrowed and his thoughts became more reasonable. He was thinking, For God's sake, take it easy. Don't blow your top again.

She was saying, "All you need to do is say the word. I'll arrange for an appointment right away."

He was able to say easily, "You really think it'll work?"

"I'm sure it will."

"Well," he said, "whichever way it goes, it's damn nice of you to try."

"Not at all." Her tone was level. "I'm only doing what

I think is fair. All this was my fault and there's no reason why you should suffer for it."

He didn't say anything. He had a relaxed feeling, an awareness that it was happening the way it should happen. Somehow it was as though they were meeting for the first time.

His smile was pleasant. "If I get my job back, it'll take a load of worry off my chest. You'll be doing me a big favor."

She had moved toward a table near the window. She put the camera on the table, then turned slightly and gazed out the window and for a few moments she didn't reply. Then, very quietly, "Maybe you'll get a chance to repay it."

He caught no special meaning from her statement, and he said lightly, "I hope so. It'll be a pleasure."

"Well," she said, moving toward the door, "we probably won't be seeing each other again."

"I guess not."

For a long moment she stood in the doorway, looking at him. Her eyes were intense, and it seemed she was trying to tell him something that she couldn't put into words.

Then very slowly she turned and walked out of the room.

Kerrigan moved toward the leather sofa. He felt the weight of heavy fatigue and it had no connection with the battering he'd taken from Ruttman. Nor was it due to the fact that he'd had less than three hours' sleep the night before. As he lowered himself to the sofa, he realized what an effort it had taken to control his anger and discuss matters calmly. It seemed to him that he'd never worked so hard in all his life . . . .

For hour after hour he slept heavily, oblivious of the loud voices of the stevedores on the pier, the clanging of chains, the thudding of crates against the planks. At a few minutes past five he was awakened by a hand shaking his shoulder, and he looked up and saw the grinning face of Ruttman.

"The front office just called," Ruttman said. "They're putting you back on the job."

Kerrigan sat up slowly, rubbing his eyes and dragging himself away from sleep.

Through a veil he heard Ruttman saying, "I'll be damned if I can figure it out. That call came from the big boss himself."

Kerrigan didn't say anything.

Ruttman was looking at him and waiting for an explanation and not getting any. The dock foreman turned away, started toward the door, then pivoted and stared at the table near the window.

Kerrigan stiffened as he saw what Ruttman was looking at. It was the camera.

"Well, whaddya know?" Ruttman breathed. "She give it to you for a gift?"

Kerrigan shook his head slowly, dazedly. "I didn't know she left it here."

Then it was quiet in the room while Ruttman walked slowly to the table and picked up the camera. He looked at it and murmured, "This ain't no ordinary gadget. If it's worth a dime, it's worth fifty bucks. Not the kind of a thing you leave around on tables."

Kerrigan's lips tightened. "What are you getting at?"

Ruttman hefted the camera in his hand. He brought it to the sofa and let it drop into Kerrigan's lap. "It's like a game of checkers," he said. "Now it's your move. You find out where she lives and you take it back to her. That's why she left it here."

The anger was coming again and he tried to hold it back but it flamed in his eyes. "The hell with her," he muttered. "I ain't running no lost-and-found department."

"You gotta take it back to her. Think it over and you'll see what I mean. If it wasn't for her, you'd be out of a job. Now you're obligated."

Ruttman turned and crossed the floor and went out of the room. Kerrigan sat there on the edge of the sofa, his hands gripping the camera. It felt like a chunk of white-hot metal, scorching the skin of his palms.

CHAPTER 9

He walked slowly along Wharf, came onto Vernon Street, then walked west on Vernon toward home. The slimy water in the gutter was lit with pink fire from the evening sun, and he looked up and saw it big and very red up there, the flares shooting out from the blazing sphere, merging with the orange clouds, so that the sky was like a huge opal, the glowing colors floating and blending, and it was really something to look at. He thought, It's tremendous. And he wondered if anyone else was looking up at it right now and thinking the same thing.

But as his gaze returned to the street he saw the dirty-faced kids playing in the gutter, he saw a drunk sprawled on a doorstep, and three middle-aged colored men sitting on the curb and drinking wine from a bottle wrapped in an old newspaper.

Under the vermilion glory of the evening sun, the vast magnificence of an opal sky, the Vernon Street citizens had no idea of what was up there, they scarcely bothered to glance up and see. All they knew was that the sun was still high, and it would be one hell of a hot night. Already the older folks were coming out of shacks and tenements to sit on doorsteps with paper fans and pitchers of water. The families who were lucky enough to have ice in the house were holding chunks of it in their mouths and trying to beat the heat that way. And a few of them, just a very few, were giving nickels to

their children, to purchase flavored ice on sticks. The
kids shrieked with glee, but their happy sound was
drowned in the greater noise, the humming noise that
was one big groan and sigh, the noise that came from
Vernon throats, yet seemed to come from the street itself.
It was as though the street had lungs and the only
sounds it could make were the groan and the sigh, the
weary acceptance of its fourth-class place in the world.
High above it there was a wondrous sky, the fabulous
colors in the orbit of the sun, but it just didn't make sense
to look up there and develop pretty thoughts and hopes
and dreams.

The realization came to Kerrigan like the sudden blow
of a hammer, putting him down on solid ground where a
spade was never anything but a spade. He looked at the
torn leather of his workshops, the calloused flesh of his
hands. He thought, You better wise up to yourself and
stay out of the clouds.

His mouth hardened. His hand moved toward the
pants pocket where he had the camera. He asked himself
what he was going to do with it.

All right, he thought, it ain't no problem. All you gotta
do is find out where she lives and mail it to her.

But he could visualize her face as she opened the package and saw the camera. He could see her lips curved in
contempt, and almost hear her saying to herself, He's
afraid to come here and ring the doorbell.

He wondered what would happen if he went up there
to the uptown street where she lived, and actually rang
the doorbell. Hell, he thought, what's there to be scared
about? Nobody's gonna bite you. But damn it, you'd be
out of place up there.

Maybe it would be all right if he looked decent, if he

was bathed and shaved and properly dressed. He needed a bath anyway, and it wasn't as though he'd be using soap just to pass some sort of test. It wouldn't hurt him to put on his Sunday clothes. There wasn't any law that said he had to wear them only on Sunday.

Maybe it would really be all right, and these uptown characters wouldn't give him any trouble. Maybe they wouldn't notice that he was different, that he didn't belong.

But no. In no time at all they'd have him sized up, they'd see him for what he was. Perhaps they'd try to be polite and not say anything, but he'd know what they were thinking. It would show in their eyes, no matter how they tried to hide it.

The thing to do, he told himself, was take this goddamn camera and throw it down a sewer or someplace. Just get rid of it.

And there it was again, the stabbing thought that he didn't have the guts to face the situation squarely. He was frightened, that was all.

He walked on down Vernon Street, wondering what to do with the camera.

Arriving at the Kerrigan house, he opened the front door and walked into the parlor. He glanced at the sofa, where Tom was snoring loudly, holding a half-empty beer bottle, the picture of utter contentment.

The only sound in the parlor was the noise coming from the kitchen, the clatter of dishes, the loud voices of Lola and Bella. At first he paid no attention to what they were saying, and his thoughts played idly with the idea that he ought to go in there and get some supper. He wondered if there was anything warm on the stove.

He started across the parlor, headed toward the

kitchen, and then he heard Bella yelling, "Just wait till I see that two-timing sneak. Wait till I get my hands on him."

"You leave him alone," Lola shouted at her daughter. "If you know what's good for you, you won't start anything."

"It's already started," Bella raged. "What do I look like, an idiot or something? You think I'll let him push me around and make a fool of me? I warned him what would happen if he messed around. I'm gonna show that louse I mean what I say."

"Not in this house you won't," Lola shouted.

"The hell I won't," Bella blazed. "And you won't stop me, neither."

There was the smacking sound of a hand against a face. He heard Bella screaming. Then another smack. And Bella screamed again.

He heard Lola say, "Talk back again and I'll slap you so hard you'll go through the wall."

Then it was quiet in the kitchen. Kerrigan decided to wait just a little longer before having supper, and perhaps Bella would be cooled off entirely by the time he was ready to eat.

He walked down the hall and into his room and took off his clothes. Then he went into the bathroom, filled the tub, and climbed in and soaped his body. In his room again, he put on a clean shirt and shorts and socks, opened the closet door and took a gray worsted suit off the hanger. It was his Sunday suit, the only suit he owned, and it needed pressing, some sewing here and there, and one of the buttons was missing. As he stood before the mirror, pulling at the lapels and trying to stretch the fabric to get rid of the wrinkles, he wished he had a better suit to wear. And while the thought ran through his mind, he was slowly lowering the camera into the jacket pocket.

He slipped a tie under his collar, knotted it three times before he was satisfied, then leaned close to the mirror and gave his wet combed hair a few final pats with his palms. Stepping back from the mirror, he studied himself from various angles, frowned appraisingly, then shrugged and decided that it would have to do.

Coming into the kitchen, he saw Lola arranging the dishes on a shelf. Bella was at the sink with a towel in her hands. The moment she saw him, her face darkened and reddened and fire came into her eyes. She took a deep breath and opened her mouth to say something. But from the other side of the room she saw her mother watching her. She took another deep breath and shut her mouth tightly and closed her eyes, grimly trying to control her temper.

Lola was smiling at Kerrigan and saying, "Want something to eat?"

He nodded and sat down at the splintered table, which had several match books under one leg to keep it balanced. Bella had turned back to the sink as if she had no idea he was in the room. But he could hear her breathing heavily and he knew she was having a hard time holding back the rage that strained to break loose.

Lola picked up a large spoon and moved majestically toward the stove. She was an excellent cook, extremely proud of it, and always anxious to prove it. She bent over the stove, studied the contents of a huge pot and a couple of smaller ones, and murmured, "It'll take just a minute to warm up."

"No hurry," Kerrigan said. He lit a cigarette and leaned back.

Lola was stirring the spoon in the pots, lifting the spoon to her mouth, testing the flavor of the beef stew and the rice and the summer squash.

"Needs pepper," Lola murmured. She looked at Bella and said, "Get me the pepper."

"Let him get it." Bella spaced the words distinctly.

"I told you to get it," Lola said.

Bella sucked air in between her teeth. She moved away from the sink, opened the kitchen cabinet, and grabbed at the pepper shaker. She brought it to the table and slammed it down in front of Kerrigan.

"Not there," Lola said. "I told you to bring it here. To me. And bring your face here so I can smack it again."

Bella swallowed hard. She was afraid to move. Kerrigan reached for the pepper shaker and handed it to Lola, who took it without looking at it. Lola aimed a dim but dangerous smile at her daughter.

"You're gonna get it," Lola said. "I can see you're itching for it, and before the night's over you're gonna get it like you never got it before. I'm telling you, girl, you got a rotten evil temper and I'm gonna knock it out of you if I have to break every bone in your body."

Bella's lips were trembling. She started toward the doorway leading out of the kitchen. Lola caught her arm, pulled her away from the doorway, then shoved her back to the sink.

"You ain't finished here yet," Lola said. "You gotta do them knives and forks. And when he's through eating, you'll have his plates to do."

Bella seemed to be choking. "Me do his plates? I gotta clean up after him?"

"You heard me," Lola said.

Kerrigan squirmed in his chair. "I can wash my own dishes."

"I said she's gonna wash them," Lola said loudly and firmly.

Kerrigan shrugged. He knew there was no use arguing with Lola.

She heaped his plate with the beef stew and the rice and the squash. She put six slices of bread on the plate, poured coffee into a thick cup, then backed away from the table and watched him tackle the meal.

Kerrigan ate slowly, chewing thoroughly, savoring each mouthful. As he sat there enjoying the meal, the kitchen was quiet except for the busy noise of his knife and fork on the plate. He completely forgot the presence of Bella, whose eyes alternated between raging glares at him and wary glances at her mother.

His plate was empty now, and Lola said, "Ready for more?"

He nodded, pushing bread into his mouth.

Lola looked at Bella and said, "Don't stand there. Pick up his plate."

Bella swallowed hard. Her voice cracked slightly as she stared pleadingly at her mother and said, "It ain't bad enough I gotta wash his dishes. Now you want me to bring him his meal. Like a servant."

Lola's eyes softened just a little. She shook her head slowly. "No," she murmured. "Not like a servant. After all, you're his woman, ain't you?"

Kerrigan winced. He looked up and studied Lola's face and all at once he knew what was in her mind. In her own blunt way she was saying to her daughter, If you want him for a husband, I'll show you how to get him.

He shifted uncomfortably in the chair. He had a strange feeling that the walls were closing in on him and he itched to get out of the house. Until now it hadn't occurred to him that Lola wanted him for a son-in-law. But as he noticed how Lola was nodding approvingly, he realized there was a plan in action, and for a fearful moment he could see himself married to Bella.

But then, as the steaming food was placed before him and he saw the smooth richness of Bella's skin, he said to himself, Why not?

He watched her as she turned away from the table, and saw how her hips moved. The construction was there, the face was there, and all he had to do was buy her a ring and he'd have all that for keeps.

Another thing. He'd soon be thirty-five and it was high time he got married. What the hell was he waiting for?

He pictured himself putting the ring on Bella's finger. He had the feeling it would settle a lot of questions that clouded his brain and circled around in there, a vague merry-go-round of issues that he just couldn't figure out. Since last night he'd been walking back and forth in a fog, doing things he didn't want to do, operating way off the beam and wondering what in God's name it was all about. Things had happened much too fast, making him dizzy, taking his feet off the ground. But there was a fast way to fix all that.

There'd be no problem in finding the right person to perform a quick ceremony. On Third Street, off Vernon, a little old Greek was capable of legally tying the knot in a matter of seconds. The Greek's son worked in City Hall, in the Marriage Bureau, and was faced with no trouble at all when it came to stealing licenses. The father and son were extremely popular in the neighborhood, for when Vernon men decided to make it legal, they didn't like to wait.

A blunt voice cut in on his thoughts. He heard Bella saying, "More coffee?"

He looked up. She was standing at the stove. He glanced around the kitchen, but Lola wasn't there and he wondered when she'd walked out of the room. Then he gazed down at his plate and saw that it was empty and he couldn't remember having finished the second helping.

"Come out of it," Bella said, and he knew she'd been watching him for some time. "I asked you if you want more coffee."

He nodded. But it wasn't for the coffee. It was just to make a reply.

Bella brought the percolator to the table and poured coffee into his cup. She poured a cup for herself and sat down across from him. Then she put cigarettes on the table and asked him if he wanted one. He nodded again, looking at her intently and trying to establish contact with her. As he leaned forward to get the light from the match she offered, he wondered what the hell was wrong here. He had the downright uncanny feeling that he wasn't here in the kitchen with Bella, he was someplace else.

"What is it?" Bella said. "What's the matter with you?"

"Nothing." He shrugged. "I had a rough day."

"You look it," she murmured. "Who slugged you?"

"It happened on the pier. It didn't last long."

"They carry him away?"

"No," he said. "They carried me."

She gave him a side glance. "How come? Lose your punch?"

He didn't say anything. He sipped at the coffee and took long drags at the cigarette and tried not to look at her. But he was focusing on her face, and seeing a parade of questions coming out of her eyes. He compared her present mood with the explosive anger of minutes ago, and realized that she'd calmed down considerably, almost to the point of passivity. He'd never seen her like this, and it made him uneasy. His throat felt tight and he worked his head from side to side, trying to loosen his collar.

"Unbutton it," she said.

"It's all right."

"Don't you feel hot? Why don't you take your jacket off?"

"I want it on." He spoke just a little louder. "You don't mind, do you?"

He was hoping she'd curse him, or say anything that would get the shouting started, their normal means of communication.

But all she said was "Of course I don't mind. I just want you to be comfortable."

"All right, I'm comfortable. You satisfied?"

She didn't reply. For some moments she just sat there looking at him. Then, in a strangely quiet tone, "I want to know why you're all dressed up."

He opened his mouth to give her an answer. His mouth stayed open but no sound came out.

Bella leaned forward, her elbows on the table. "Come on, let's have it. You might as well tell me who she is. I've seen her already."

He blinked a few times.

"Last night," Bella said. "I was in bed, waiting for you. When you didn't come in, I got up to see what you were doing. I went into the parlor and took a look through the front window. I saw you talking to her. And then the two of you got into the car and drove away."

He managed to look away from her. "It wasn't what you think."

Her face was expressionless. "I haven't told you what I think. I'm waiting to hear what your plans are."

"What plans?"

Bella's eyes were drills going into him. "You and her."

"For God's sake!" He shouted it, and jumped up from the table. "What are you building here? That broad don't mean a thing to me. I hardly even know her!"

He jammed his hands into his trousers pockets and started to walk up and down alongside the table.

"Another thing," Bella said. "You didn't come home last night. I stayed up, waiting for you. Where'd you go? Where'd you sleep?"

The floor seemed to be moving under his feet and he wished it would keep on moving and take him away from all these questions he couldn't handle. But the floor kept him there near the table, holding him on the track, setting him there like a slowly moving target while the sharpshooter took aim.

Then Bella shot it at him. "Whoever she is, she's doing something to you. She's got you wrapped around her finger."

It was like a crowbar hitting him in the eyes. He backed away from the table, staring at Bella. "What gives you that crazy idea?"

"I can tell. It's plastered all over your face."

He took several deep breaths. But that didn't help. He turned his back to the table, folded his arms, and glowered at the floor.

And he heard Bella saying, "You see what I mean? It shows. You can't even look me in the eye."

For the moment he wished he were one of the smooth talkers, the con artists who could handle this sort of thing and slide out of it without any trouble. But then, as he pivoted hard and faced her, he was glaring and his voice was blunt. "Now listen," he said. "I'll tell you once and then it's ended, you hear? There ain't a goddamn thing happening with me and that chippy. She's one of them phonys from uptown. She came down here to play around and get some kicks. All I did was tell her off and send her on her way."

Bella's features were impassive. Then gradually a smile worked its way onto her lips, a perceptive smile that narrowed her eyes as she murmured, "She's got you so mixed up, you're dizzy. You really go for her."

"Sure," he snarled. "Like a fish goes for dry land. You don't know what the hell you're talking about."

"Don't I?" Bella slowly arose from the table. She looked him up and down. She smiled and said, "This tickles me. It's really very funny."

He stiffened. "What's funny?"

Her smile was pure disdain. "You," she said. "You're the comedian. And what takes the cake is that getup you're wearing. Making a social call uptown?" She started to laugh at him.

"Stop it," he said.

She went on laughing.

He stood rigid and his fists were clenched and he spoke through his teeth. "Goddamn you," he said. "Stop it."

"I can't." She was holding her sides, as though her ribs were cracking. Her laughter climbed to a screaming pitch.

Kerrigan moved toward her, his eyes burning, his teeth grinding. But suddenly he stopped short, staring past Bella, seeing something that caused him to stiffen. His eyes were aiming at a small mirror on the wall and he saw his carefully combed hair and the Sunday suit.

The mocking laughter jabbed at him like hot needles inserted in his brain. But he heard it, the jeering sound wasn't coming from Bella. He told himself it came from the mirror.

He turned away and hurried out of the kitchen. The laughter followed him down the hall, through the parlor, and went on jabbing at him as he opened the front door and walked out of the house.

CHAPTER 10

He walked aimlessly on Vernon, crossing the street several times for no good reason at all. On Wharf Street he turned around and went back on Vernon all the way to Eleventh, then walked eleven blocks back to Wharf, and turned around again. It didn't occur to him how much ground he was covering, how many hours it was taking. The only definite feeling he had was the weight of the camera in his jacket pocket.

The sky was dark now. He continued to walk back and forth along Vernon Street and finally he stood outside a store window, staring at the face of a clock that read eleven-forty. He scowled at the clock and asked himself what in hell he was going to do with the camera.

He turned away from the store window and resumed walking along Vernon. The heat-weary citizens were grouped on doorsteps, the perspiration gleaming on their faces. As Kerrigan walked past, they stared at him in wonder, seeing the buttoned collar and the necktie and the heavy worsted jacket and trousers. They shook their heads.

But although he wasn't thinking about it, the sticky heat seeped into his body and he moved with increasing difficulty. His mouth and throat were aching for a cold drink. He saw the light in the window of Dugan's Den, and it occurred to him that he could use a few beers.

Entering the taproom, he heard the squeaky tune that

Dugan hummed off key. There were three customers at the bar, a couple of hags with a lot of rouge on their faces and an ageless humpbacked derelict bent low over a glass of wine. The hags were glaring at Dugan, who had his arms folded and his eyes half closed and was concentrating on the music that came from his lips.

One of the hags leaned toward Dugan and yelled, "Shut up with that noise. I can't stand that goddamn noise."

Dugan went on humming.

"You gonna shut up?" the hag screeched.

"He won't shut up," the other hag said. "Only way to quiet him down is shoot him."

"One of these nights I'll do just that," the first hag said. "I'll come in here with a gun, and so help me, I'll put a slug in his throat."

Kerrigan was at the bar. He caught Dugan's attention and said he wanted a beer. Dugan filled a glass and brought it to him. He finished it quickly and ordered another. He looked up at the clock above the bar and the hands pointed to twelve-ten. In his jacket pocket the camera was very heavy.

The first hag was pointing to Kerrigan and saying loudly, "Look at that goddamn fool. Look at the way he's all dressed up."

"In a winter suit," the other hag said.

"Maybe he thinks it's wintertime," the first hag said. She was short and shapeless and her hair was dyed orange.

The other hag began to laugh. She made a sound like two pieces of rusty metal scraping against each other. Her throat was ribboned with several knife scars and on her face she had a hideous vertical scar that ran from the right eye down to the mouth. She was of average height and weighed around eighty pounds. Pointing a bony finger at Kerrigan, she jeered, "You tryin' to suffocate? Is that whatcha wanna do? You wanna suffocate?"

"He don't even hear ya," the shapeless hag said. "He's all dressed up to go somewhere and he don't even hear ya."

"Hey, stupid," the scarred woman hollered. "You goin' to a party? Take us with you."

"Yeah. We're all dressed up, too."

Kerrigan looked at them. He saw the rags they wore, the cracked leather and broken heels of their shoes. Then he looked at their faces and he recognized them. The shapeless woman with orange hair was named Frieda and she lived in a shack a few doors away from the Kerrigan house. The scarred woman was the widow of a ditchdigger and her name was Dora. Both women were in their early forties and he'd known them since his childhood.

"Hello, Frieda," he said. "Hello, Dora."

They stiffened and stared at him.

"Don't you know me?" he said.

Without moving from where they stood at the other end of the bar, they leaned forward to get a better look at him.

"I know what he is," Frieda said. "He's a federal."

Dora slanted her head and looked Kerrigan up and down and then she nodded slowly.

"A goddamn federal," Frieda said. "I can spot them a mile away."

"What's he want with us?" Dora's voice was wary.

"I'm wise to these federals," Frieda declared in a loud voice. "They can't put anything over on me. Hey, you," she shouted at Kerrigan. "Whatever you got in mind, forget it. We ain't bootleggers and we ain't peddling dope. We're honest, hard-working women and we go to church and we're all paid up on our income taxes."

"And another thing," Dora cut in. "We're not counterfeiters."

"We're decent citizens," Frieda stated. Her voice climbed to a shrill blast. "You leave us alone, you hear?"

Kerrigan sighed and went back to his beer. He knew there was no use trying to prove his identity. He knew that Frieda and Dora were mixing their fear of the law with a certain pleasure, a feeling of importance. They visualized the United States government sending an agent to deal with two clever queens of vice. But they'd show him. They'd trip him up on every move he made.

He called to Dugan and said he was buying drinks for the ladies. They ordered double shots of gin and didn't bother to thank him because they were in a hurry to get it down. And when it was down they forgot all about him; they gazed at the empty glasses and tried to drown themselves in the emptiness.

While Dugan hummed the squeaky tune, Kerrigan leaned low over the bar, not hearing it. He was gazing at the half-empty glass of beer and feeling the weight of the camera in his pocket.

Then the door opened and someone came into the taproom. The women looked around at the newcomer, who smiled a quietly amiable greeting and moved toward a table at the other side of the room. The hags made oaths without sound as they glowered at the delicately chiseled face of Newton Channing. He was wearing a clean white shirt and a light summer suit that was freshly pressed. As he seated himself at a table he lit a cigarette with a green enamel-cased lighter. It sent a pale green glow onto his thin, sensitive features and gave a greenish tint to his yellow hair.

The two hags went on looking at Newton Channing, their eyes reflecting a mixture of curiosity and absurdly futile envy.

Kerrigan had raised his head and he was staring at the mirror behind the bar. He watched the smoke climbing languidly from the cigarette in Channing's mouth. His hand moved slowly along the side of his jacket and he reached into the pocket containing the camera.

He waited until Dugan served Channing a water glass filled with whisky. Then he walked across the room to Channing's table. He took the camera out of his pocket and put it on the table.

"What's this?" Channing asked without interest.

"It belongs to your sister."

"Where'd you get it?"

"She left it with me."

Channing frowned slightly. He picked up the camera and turned it around in his hands, holding it close to his eyes and giving it a careful inspection. Then he put it down and his head turned slowly and he looked at Kerrigan.

He said, "Aren't you the man I met last night?"

Kerrigan nodded. "You bought me a beer. We talked for a while."

"Yes, I remember." Channing turned his attention back to the camera. "What's the story on this?"

Kerrigan laughed.

"What's funny?" Channing asked. His voice was very soft.

Kerrigan moved to the other side of the table and sat

down. Channing had pushed the glass of whisky aside and was leaning forward and frowning puzzledly, his eyes still on the camera.

Kerrigan drummed his fingers on the tabletop. He said, "You better have a talk with your sister. Tell her she was very lucky this time. Maybe next time she won't be so lucky."

Channing looked at him. "I don't know what you mean."

"Can't you add it up?"

Channing shook his head. His eyes were blank.

"She made a play for me," Kerrigan said. He leaned back in the chair and waited for Channing's reaction.

But there was no reaction, except that the puzzlement faded just a little. And then Channing shrugged. He reached out for the water glass filled with whisky, lifted it to his mouth, and took a long drink. Then he put the cigarette to his lips and pulled at it easily. The smoke came out of his nose and mouth like the smoke from an incense burner, thin columns climbing lazily.

Kerrigan could feel himself stiffening. He tried to loosen up, but his eyes were getting hard and his voice sounded tight and strained. "Didn't you hear what I said? She made a play for me."

"So?"

"You don't seem to care."

"Why should I?"

Kerrigan spoke with bitter sarcasm. "She's got class. You don't want her mixing with bar flies and dock workers."

"I don't give a damn who she mixes with."

"She's your sister," Kerrigan said. "Don't she mean anything to you?"

"She means a great deal to me. I'm awfully fond of Loretta."

"Then why don't you look out for her?"

"She's old enough to look out for herself."

"Not after dark. Not in this neighborhood. No woman is safe in this neighborhood."

Channing lifted his gaze from the camera and studied Kerrigan's face. For some moments he didn't speak. Then he said quietly, "I'm not worried. Why should you be?"

It was a perfectly logical statement. Kerrigan swallowed hard and said, "Just trying to give you advice, that's all."

"Thank you," Channing said. He slanted his head a little. "I think you're the one who needs advice."

Kerrigan found himself staring toward the center of the table, at the camera.

He heard Channing saying, "Don't be afraid of her."

It seemed to him that the tabletop was coming up to hit him in the face. He pulled his head to one side. He wondered why he couldn't look at Channing.

"There's no reason to be afraid," Channing said. "After all, she's just a woman."

He tried to reply. He groped for phrases and couldn't find a single word.

"I'm saying this," Channing murmured, "because I know you want her."

"You're crazy."

"Possibly," Channing admitted with complete gravity. "But at times it's the lunatic who makes the most sense. Maybe you're not aware that you want her, but it shows in your eyes. You want her very much and you're terribly afraid of her."

Something tugged at Kerrigan's throat. He spoke in a

whisper. "Sure I'm afraid. I'm afraid if she bothers me again I might clip her in the teeth."

Channing raised his eyebrows. For a long moment he was quietly thoughtful. Then he said, "Well, that's easily understandable. From your point of view she's just fooling around."

Kerrigan put his hands flat on the table. His palms pressed hard against the wood. He didn't say anything.

Channing said, "It's quite possible she's more serious than you think. Why don't you try to find out?"

"I'm not interested. Happens I got something else on my mind."

He paused, waiting for it to sink in.

Channing's face was impassive.

"It concerns you." And there was another pause, much longer. "I'd like to find out more about you."

"Me?" Channing frowned. "What for? Any special reason?"

"I think you know what the reason is. I'm not ready to say for sure. But I think you know."

Channing's eyebrows were up again. "That sounds rather sinister. Now you have me curious."

"Not worried?"

"No. Just curious."

"You ought to be worried."

Channing smiled. "I never worry. I suffer a lot, but I never worry." He reached for the glass of whisky. He took a very long drink, emptying the glass. Then he poured more whisky from the bottle and took another drink. He said, "I wish you'd tell me what this is all about."

"I'm not ready to tell you."

Channing went on smiling. It was a relaxed smile.

"I hope it's something exciting," he murmured. "I like excitement."

"That's what I figured," Kerrigan said. "Anything for kicks."

"Sure." Channing lit another cigarette. "Why not?" He took an easy drag, let it go down deep, and then it came out in little clouds as he said, "A few weeks ago I thought it would be nice to see Alaska. I'd never been to Alaska and I had this sudden notion to make the trip. The idea hit me on a Wednesday afternoon. An hour later I was in a plane. Thursday night I was making love to a sixty-year-old Eskimo woman."

For some moments Kerrigan was silent. Then he said, "How was it in Alaska?"

"Very nice. Rather cold, but really very nice."

Kerrigan's hands were still flat on the table. He looked down at them. "You do these things often?"

"Now and then," Channing said. "Depends on what mood I'm in."

"I bet you have all kinds of moods."

"Hundreds of them," Channing admitted. He laughed without sound. "I ought to keep a filing cabinet. It's hard to remember such a wide variety."

Kerrigan closed his eyes and for a moment all he saw was black. And then something happened to the blackness and it became the dark alley and the dried bloodstains.

He could feel the trembling that began in his chest and went up to his brain and down to his chest again. His eyes were open now and he stared at his hands and saw that his knuckles were white. He said to himself, Cut it out, you're not sure yet, you don't have proof, you can't do anything if you don't have proof.

Just then something caused him to turn his head and he saw the two hags who stood at the bar. They were making hissing sounds and their eyes were focused on him and Channing. And then, somewhat hesitantly, they moved toward the table.

They approached the table with their faces sullen and belligerent and yet their twisted mouths seemed to be pleading for something. Frieda was trying to wriggle her shapeless hips and her hands made dainty adjustments to her orange hair. Dora swayed her bony shoulders and attempted to show the curves of a body that had no curves. As the two of them came closer, it was like a walking bag of flour and a walking broomstick.

"Get the hell away," Kerrigan muttered.

"We've got a right to sit down," Dora said. And then she recognized him. "Well, whaddya know? It's Bill Kerrigan."

"Damn if it ain't," Frieda shouted.

"And he's all dressed up in his Sunday best," Dora declared. She let out a high-pitched, jarring laugh. "We thought you was a federal." She folded her arms and unfolded them and then folded them again. "Why the special outfit?"

"This here's a special table," Frieda said. She made a gesture to indicate Channing, who sat there relaxed and smiling dimly.

Dora had stopped laughing and her face was pleated with lines curving downward. "It may be special, but it ain't reserved. If they can sit here, so can we."

"You're goddamn right," Frieda said. She took the chair next to Channing. Then she shifted the chair so that the grimy fabrics covering her hip came up against the side of his clean jacket.

Dora sat down beside Kerrigan. She put her arm around his shoulder. He cursed without sound, took hold of her wrist, and pushed her arm away. But then her arm was there again. He said, "what the hell," and let it stay there.

"Gonna buy us a drink?" Frieda asked Channing.

"Why, certainly," Channing said. "What would you like?"

"Gin," Dora said. "We don't drink nothing but gin."

Channing called to Dugan and said he wanted a bottle of gin and two glasses. At the bar the humpbacked wino had turned and was looking at the table. The face of the wino was expressionless.

"Would you like something?" Channing asked the wino.

"Go to hell," the wino said. He said it with an effort. There was no more wine in his glass and he had seven cents in his pocket and wine was fifteen. He took a deep dragging breath and said, "You can go to hell."

"Same to you," Frieda yelled at the wino. "We want no part of you, you humpbacked freak."

"Don't say that," Channing said mildly. "That isn't nice."

Frieda twisted in her chair and glowered at him. "Don't you tell me how to talk. I'm a lady and I know how to talk."

"All right," Channing said.

"We're both ladies, me and my friend Dora. That's Dora there. My name's Frieda."

"Pleased to meet you," he said. "I'm Newton Channing."

Frieda spoke loudly. "We don't give a damn who you are. You ain't no better than us." She sat up very straight, and her eyes were hard. "What makes you think you're better than us?"

"Is that what I think?"

"Sure," Dora said. "You ain't kidding nobody."

Channing shrugged. Dugan arrived at the table with the bottle of gin and two glasses. Channing looked at Kerrigan. "What's yours?"

"I don't want anything," Kerrigan mumbled. "I'm getting out of here." He tried to twist away from the pressure of Dora's skinny arm. She put her other arm around him and held him there.

He didn't hear the sound of the door and he didn't hear the approaching footsteps in his struggle to pull away from Dora. Then something caused him to look up and he saw her standing at the side of the table, he saw the lovely face and golden hair of Loretta Channing.

She was looking at him. Her gaze was intent and she was ignoring the others at the table.

Frieda said, "Who's this tramp?"

"This tramp," Channing said, "is my sister."

"She ain't bad-looking," Dora commented.

"What's she doin' here?" Frieda asked. "She lookin' for a pickup?"

"There's one over there," Dora said, and pointed to the humpback at the bar. "Go on over and talk to him," she told Loretta. She didn't like the way Loretta was looking at Kerrigan. Her arm pressed tighter around Kerrigan's shoulder and she spoke louder. "Can't ya see we're teamed up here? Ya can't sit here unless you're with a man."

Loretta went on looking at Kerrigan.

Dora began to breathe hard. "All right, you," she hissed at Loretta. "You quit puttin' your eye on him. He's with me. Ya wanna see him, ya gotta see me first."

"That's right, tell her," Frieda said.

Channing was chuckling. "Be careful, Dora. My sister packs a punch."

"She don't worry me," Dora said. "She starts with me, she'll need nurses day and night."

She saw that Loretta was ignoring her and continuing to look at Kerrigan. She stood up and put her face close to Loretta's face and shouted, "Now listen, you, I told you to stop lookin' at him."

"Don't shout in my face," Loretta said quietly.

"You keep it up and I'll spit in your face."

Loretta smiled. Her eyes stayed on Kerrigan as she murmured, "No, don't do that."

"You dare me?" Dora screeched.

"Sure she dares you," Channing said. "Can't you see she's looking for trouble?"

"Well, sure as hell she's gonna get it," Dora stated. "When I'm with a man I don't want no floozie buttin' in."

Loretta looked at the skinny hag. "You're right," she said. "You're absolutely right. I'm very sorry." She backed away from Dora and then turned and walked toward the bar.

But Dora wasn't satisfied. Dora yelled, "You don't get off that easy, you tramp." She lowered her head and went lunging across the room. At the last moment Loretta stepped to one side and Dora collided with the bar and bounced back and landed flat on the floor. She rolled over on her side, tried to get up, and tripped over her own legs and went down again. She made another attempt to rise, managed to get on her feet, and saw Loretta standing with hands on hips, waiting for her. There was something in Loretta's eyes that told Dora to think in terms of personal safety.

As Dora backed away from Loretta, the humpbacked

wino let out a quiet laugh of disdain. Dora whirled on the wino and began to blast him with a stream of curses. Loretta turned away from them and told Dugan she wanted whisky. At the table, Frieda was telling Channing that he ought to get himself a wife and settle down. She began to speak in low tones, discussing the various benefits of matrimony. Channing had turned in his chair to face her and give her his undivided attention. Frieda declared that every man needed a woman to live with, that in order to preserve one's health it was necessary to lead a wholesome domestic life. Channing agreed with her. He said he was definitely in favor of a wholesome domestic life. He asked Frieda what her age was, and she said forty-three. Channing nodded thoughtfully and then he asked her what she weighed and she said one-seventy. He told her that one-seventy was all right and then he asked her if she knew how to cook. She said no. Channing's eyes were steady and level on the shapeless hag with orange hair. His voice was serious as he told her that she might as well start learning how to cook.

Kerrigan sat there and listened to it and he was staring at the camera. He heard Frieda saying, "You mean it?" and Channing said, "Yes, Frieda," and then Frieda said, "Well, I'll be goddamned." Kerrigan was trying to drag his eyes away from the camera. He told himself to get up and get out of here. He heard the ginrusty voice of Frieda as she said, "You mean I'll actually be your wife and you'll be my husband?" Without the slightest hesitation, Channing answered, "Absolutely, if that's what you'd like." Kerrigan took hold of the table edge and tried to lift himself from the chair, but the lens of the camera had hold of his eyes and he couldn't move.

Frieda was saying, "When do we do it?" and Channing said, "You set the date."

The legs of Kerrigan's chair scraped the floor, and then he was up from the table. He looked down at the shapeless hag and said, "Why do you let him tease you?"

Frieda gazed up at him. Her mouth sagged. "Is that what he's doing?" She turned her head to study Channing's face. She said, "You just sittin' here and havin' fun with me?"

Channing was pouring more whisky into his glass. He took a long, slow drink, the equivalent of three shots. He said, "I told you to set the date."

Kerrigan scowled at Frieda and said, "You damn fool. Can't you see he's pulling your leg? He's making you pay for the gin. Only thing he wants is entertainment."

"Aw, dry up," Frieda said. "I ain't askin' for your opinion." She turned to Channing and smiled fondly at him. There was some sadness in the smile. "It's all right, I know it's just a gag. I know you can't really mean it."

"But I do mean it," Channing said. His voice was soft, his eyes were tender. He spoke to her as though Kerrigan weren't there. "Believe me," he said. "Try to believe me."

Kerrigan snorted. He pulled away from the table and turned toward the door. He took a step in that direction and then he saw Loretta at the bar on the other side of the room. He stood motionless, looking at her as she leaned over the bar. Gradually his eyes narrowed. He went back to the table and picked up the camera. He walked slowly across the room and came up beside her and put the camera on the bar.

He said matter-of-factly, "You left this in the pier office."

He was turning to leave. She put her hand on his arm. "Please don't go."

"I have a date."

She looked him up and down. "Is that why you're all dressed up?"

He didn't reply.

For a long moment she studied his eyes. Then she said, "Of course you have a date. With me."

"Since when?"

"Since you took a bath and shaved and put on your best clothes."

He frowned. "I didn't do it for you."

She slanted her head, regarding him from a side angle. "For who else would you do it?"

He opened his mouth to give her a fast vicious answer, but no words came out. He waited for her to let go of his arm so he could walk away from her. Then he realized she wasn't holding his arm, she'd released it several moments ago. He wondered why he had the feeling she was still holding onto his arm.

Behind the bar Dugan was waiting to be paid for a whisky and water. Loretta opened her purse and took out a dollar bill and gave it to him. He gave her the change, two quarters and two dimes. The transaction was made without haste and Kerrigan wished they'd speed it up. He couldn't understand his impatience. For some unaccountable reason he was in a hurry, and it was as though he couldn't move unless she moved along with him.

He stood there and waited while she put the seventy cents in her purse and slipped the purse into her skirt pocket. He shifted his weight from one foot to the other and watched her sipping the whisky and water. She sipped it slowly, and without sound he said, Come on, come on. She turned and looked at him. She placed the glass on the table, picked up the camera, and smiled at him as she murmured, "I'm ready now, if you are."

The floor seemed to slide under his feet, taking him away from the bar. The ceiling moved backward and the walls moved and the door came closer. Behind him there was the sound of Dora's shrill voice as she went on yapping at the humpbacked wino. And the sound of lower voices, the continued conversation of Frieda and Channing. And also the sound of a squeaky tune that came humming from the lips of Dugan. But all the sounds were meaningless, a chorus adding up to nothing. What he heard was a roaring in his brain as he walked with Loretta toward the door, and past the door, and out of Dugan's Den.

CHAPTER 11

He stood with her on the corner outside the tap-room. He saw the little sport car parked across the street. It was clean and shiny, and the moonlight seemed to give it a silvery gleam. It glimmered like a jewel against the shabby background of shacks and tenements. He thought, It don't belong here, it just don't fit in with the picture.

He looked at Loretta. She was waiting for him to say something. He swallowed hard and mumbled, "Wanna go for a walk?"

"Let's use the car."

They crossed the street and climbed into the MG. She started the engine. He leaned back in the seat and tried to make himself comfortable. He felt very uncomfortable and it had nothing to do with the seating arrangement. She saw him squirming and she said, "It's such a tiny car. There isn't much room."

"It's all right," he said. But it wasn't all right. He told himself he didn't belong in the car. He wanted to open the door and get out. He wondered why he couldn't get out.

The car was moving. He said, "Where we going?"

"Any place you'd like. Would you care to ride up-town?"

He shook his head abruptly.

"Why not?" she asked.

He didn't have an answer. He had his arms folded and he was staring straight ahead.

"I can show you where I live," she said.

"No." His voice was gruff.

"It isn't far away," she urged mildly. "Just a short ride. Not even twenty minutes."

"I don't want to go there."

"Any special reason?"

Again he couldn't answer.

She said, "It's very nice uptown."

"I bet it is." He spoke between his teeth. "A damn sight nicer than it is down here."

"That isn't what I meant."

"I know what you meant." His hands put a tight grip on the edge of the seat. "Do me a favor, will you? Quit trying to put things on an equal basis. You're from up there and I'm from down here. Let's leave it that way."

"But that doesn't make sense. That's stupid."

"All right, it's stupid. But that's the way it is. So just drive toward the river."

The car moved faster. It came onto Wharf Street and he told her to turn north for several blocks and presently he told her to park up ahead. He pointed to a wide gap between the piers. It was a grassy slope, slanting down to the water's edge.

It was mostly weeds and moss, not much more than a mud flat, and during the day it was nothing to see. But under the moon it was serene and pastoral, the tall weeds somehow stately and graceful, like ferns.

"Very pretty," she murmured. "It's nice here."

"Well, it's quiet, anyway. And there's a breeze."

For some moments they didn't say anything. He wondered why he'd directed her to this place. It occurred to him that he used to come here when he was a kid, coming here alone to feel the quiet and get the river breeze. Or maybe just to get away from the shacks and the tenements.

He heard her saying, "It's so different here. Like a little island, away from everything." Then he looked at her. The moonlight poured onto her golden hair and put lights in her eyes. Her face was entrancing. He could taste the nectar of her nearness.

He told himself he wanted her, he had to have her. The need was so intense that he wondered what kept him from taking her into his arms. Then all at once he knew what it was. It was something deeper than hunger of the flesh. He wanted to reach her heart, her spirit. And his brain seethed with bitterness as he thought, That ain't what she wants. All she's out for is a cheap thrill.

The bitterness showed in his eyes. He spoke thickly. "Start the car. Let's get away from here."

"Why?" She frowned slightly. "What's wrong?"

He couldn't look at her. "You're just fooling around. Having yourself a good time."

"That isn't true."

"The hell it isn't. I been around enough to know what the score is."

"You're adding it up backward."

"Am I?" He glowered at her. "Who do you think you're kidding?"

She didn't say anything, just shook her head slowly.

He pointed to the key dangling from the ignition lock. "Come on, start the car."

She didn't budge. Her hands were folded loosely in her lap. She looked down at them and said quietly,

"You're not giving me much of a chance."

"Chance for what?" His voice was jagged. "To play me for a goddamn fool?"

She looked at him. "Why do you say these things?"

"I'm only saying what I think."

"You sure about that? You really know what you're thinking?"

"I know when I'm being taken. I know that I don't like to be jerked around."

"You don't trust me?"

"Sure I trust you. As far as I could throw a ten-ton truck."

She smiled again, but there was pain in her eyes. "Well, anyway, I tried."

He frowned. "Tried what?"

"Something I've never done before. It isn't a woman's nature to do the chasing. Not openly, anyway. But I knew it was the only way I could get to know you." She shrugged. "I'm sorry you're not interested."

His frown deepened. "This on the level?"

She didn't reply. She just looked at him.

"Damn it," he murmured, "you got me all mixed up. Now I don't know what to think."

She went on in a tone of self-reproach, "I tried to be subtle. Or clever. Or whatever it was. Like today on the docks, when I used the camera. But deep inside myself I knew the real reason I wanted your picture."

He looked away from her.

She said very quietly, "I wanted to keep you with me. I had to settle for a snapshot. But later, when I left the camera on the table, I was strictly a female playing a game. What I should have done was say it openly, bluntly."

118   DAVID GOODIS

"Say what?"

"I want you."

He could feel his brain spinning. He fought the dizziness and managed to say, "I'm not in the market for a one-night stand."

"I didn't mean it that way. You know I didn't mean it that way."

For some moments he couldn't speak. He was trying to adjust his thoughts. Finally he said, "This is happening too fast. We hardly know each other."

"What's there to know? Is it so important to find out all the details? The moment I met you, I felt something. It was a feeling I've never had before. That's all I want to know. That feeling."

"Yes," he said. "I know. I know just what you mean."

"You feel it too?"

"Yes."

They sat there in the bucket seats of the MG, and the space between the seats was a gap between them. Yet it seemed they were embracing each other. Without moving, without touching her, he caressed her eyes and her lips, and heard her saying, "This is all I want. Just this. Just being near you."

"Loretta—"

"Yes?"

"Don't go away."

"I won't."

"I mean, never go away. Never."

She sighed. Her eyes were closed. She murmured, "If you really mean it."

"Yes," he said. "I want this to last."

"It will," she said. "I know it will."

But it wasn't her words that he heard. It was like soft

music drifting through the dream. And the dream was taking him away from everything he'd known, every tangible segment of the world he lived in. It took him away from the cracked plaster walls of the Kerrigan house, the noises of the tenants in the crowded rooms upstairs, the yelling and bawling and cursing. It took him away from the raucous voice of Lola, and the empty beer bottles cluttering the parlor, and his father snoozing on the sofa. And in the dream there was a voice that said good-by to Tom, good-by to the house, good-by to Vernon Street. It was a murmur of farewell to the tenements and the shacks, the thick dust on the pavements, the vacant lots littered with rubbish, the yowling of cats in dark alleys. But there was one dark alley that refused to accept the farewell. Like an exhibit on wheels it came rolling into the dream to show the rutted paving, the moonlight a relentless lamp glow focused on some dried bloodstains.

His eyes narrowed to focus on the kin of the number-one suspect.

His voice was toneless. "Tell me something."

But he didn't know how to take it from there. It was like a tug of war in his brain. One side ached to hold onto the dream. The other side was reality, somber and grim. His sister was asleep in a grave and she'd put herself there because a man had invaded her flesh and crushed her spirit. He told himself he had to find the man. Regardless of everything else, he had to find the man and exact full payment. His hands trembled, wanting to take hold of an unseen throat.

She was waiting for him to speak. She sat there smiling at him.

He stared past her. "You like your brother?"

"Very much. He's a drunkard and a loafer and very eccentric, but sometimes he can be very nice. Why do you ask?"

"I been puzzled about him." He looked at her. "I been wondering why he comes to Dugan's Den."

For some moments she didn't reply. Then, with a slight shrug, "It's just a place where he can hide."

"What's he hiding from?"

"From himself."

"I don't get that."

Suddenly her eyes were clouded. She looked away from him. "Let's not talk about it."

"Why not?"

"It isn't pleasant." But then, with a quick shake of her head, "No, I'm wrong. You have every right to know."

She told him about her family. It was a small family, just her parents and her brother and herself. An ordinary middle-class family in fairly comfortable circumstances. But her mother liked to drink and her father had his own bedroom. She said they were dead now, so it didn't matter if she talked about them. They had an intense dislike for each other. It was so intense that they never even bothered to quarrel, they hardly ever spoke to each other. One night, when her brother was seventeen and had just got his driver's license, he took their parents out for a ride. He came home alone with a bandage around his head. The father had died instantly and the mother died in the hospital. Within a few weeks Newton began to have fits of hysterical laughter, wondering aloud if he'd done it on purpose, actually doing them a favor and giving them an easy way out. A bachelor uncle came to take charge of the house but couldn't put up with Newton's ravings and strange behaviour and finally moved out.

When Newton was nineteen he married the house-keeper, a woman in her middle forties. She was a short and very skinny woman and her face was dreadfully scarred from burns in a childhood accident. No man had ever looked twice at her and she did her best to please Newton but that wasn't what he wanted. He wanted her to be harsh and nasty and downright vicious. He was always trying to agitate her, trying to make her lose her temper. Whenever that happened he seemed delighted, especially when she'd claw him or throw dishes at him. After seven years she couldn't take it any more and she went to a lawyer and got a divorce. A few months later Newton married a Hungarian gypsy, a fortuneteller, a tall bony, beak-nosed woman who already had several husbands in various parts of the nation. She was in her early fifties and used liquid shoe polish to keep her hair black. Sometimes she'd get very thirsty and drink the shoe polish. At other times she forced Newton to give her large sums of money so she could buy cases of expensive bourbon. He had an income of sixty dollars a week from his father's insurance money and some weeks the entire sixty dollars went for liquor. Loretta was working in a dental laboratory and making forty a week and couldn't keep much for herself because Newton and the gypsy woman were always asking for money.

When Loretta was twenty, she married a young dentist. For a while they lived in a small apartment. But she was always worried about Newton, she had a feeling there was a bombshell in him and sooner or later it would burst. Her husband kept telling her to forget about Newton but she couldn't do it, and eventually she insisted on moving back to the house. He refused. They argued. The arguments became worse. Finally he walked out on her. She blamed herself, and got in touch with him, told him she was sorry, and asked him to come back. But she didn't really want him back. By this time she was very confused and she wasn't sure what she wanted. She was really relieved when the dentist told her it was no use trying a reconciliation, he cared for her very much but he had enough sense to know when a thing was ended. He advised her to get a divorce. She got the divorce and went back to live in the house with Newton and the gypsy woman.

It wasn't easy, living there with them. They were drunk most of the time, the gypsy woman made no attempt to keep the house clean, and the sink was always stacked with dirty dishes. There were empty bottles all over the place. Sometimes the gypsy woman would hurl the bottles at Newton's head. At other times she'd try to crack his ribs with a broom handle. On one occasion she hit him very hard and broke two of his ribs. He sat on the floor, grinning at her, telling her that she was a fine woman and he adored her.

Loretta told herself she couldn't stay in this madhouse. But she had to stay. She had to look after Newton. He was getting worse, drinking more and more. One time he went out and purchased a skeleton costume. In the middle of the night the gypsy woman heard a noise in the room and woke up and saw the skeleton and began to scream at the top of her lungs. The skeleton moved toward her, laughing crazily, and she passed out cold. After that night, she walked around with a blank look in her eyes. Some weeks later she caught cold, neglected it, developed pneumonia, and died. At the funeral Newton had another of his laughing spells. Then, for some months, he was all right and he got a job in an agency selling foreign automobiles. He worked very hard, and kept away from liquor. He was extremely considerate of Loretta, and extravagantly generous. For Christmas he gave her the little British car, the MG. They had a very nice Christmas dinner, just the two of them. He was gracious and quietly gallant. She was so thankful, the way he was behaving these days. She was so proud of him. But less than a week later he had another laughing spell. And the next day he quit his job. And then he began to drink again.

"When was that?" Kerrigan asked.

"About a year ago."

"When'd he start coming to Dugan's?"

"Just about then."

He told himself to continue the questions. But something stopped him. It was the expression on her face. Her eyes were dry and yet it seemed she was weeping.

"Don't," he said. "Don't look so sad."

She tried to smile, but her lips trembled.

He said, "I know it ain't been easy for you."

Her head was lowered. She put her hand to her eyes.

Suddenly he felt the pain she was feeling. His brain pushed aside all thought of Newton Channing, all aspects of the grim issue he'd been trying to settle. The only thing he knew was the yearning to hold her and hold her and never let her go.

And again he was immersed in the dream that took him away from Vernon Street.

His voice was a husky whisper. "Look at me."

She took her hand away from her eyes.

He said, "I want to take care of you. From now on."

Her lips were parted. She held her breath.

"For keeps," he said.

She was staring at him. "You know what you're saying?"

He nodded slowly. But his thoughts were spinning and there was the flashing of a warning light. He didn't know what it meant. He told himself he didn't want to know.

"It's gotta be for keeps," he said. "It can't be any other way." And then blindly, in a frenzy of wanting her, needing her, he reached out and took hold of her wrists. His voice was a hoarse whisper. "We won't quit. We'll do it tonight."

"Tonight?"

His eyes were feverish. "I know where we can get a license."

"But—"

"Just say yes. Say it."

She went on staring at him. Then very slowly she turned her head and gazed out past the shoreline, looking at the moonlight on the river. For a long moment the only sound was the lapping of the water along the bank.

And then there was the sound of her voice saying, "Yes."

CHAPTER 12

He didn't move. It was a kind of paralysis, as though he'd been hit on the skull with a sledgehammer, just hard enough to put him in a daze. The air became a tunnel of mist.

"Well?" she said.

He flinched. Again he sensed the flashing of the signal light. But now it didn't give a warning. Instead it offered the blunt message: Too late now, you're in it up to your neck, there's no way out.

His lips moved mechanically. He told her to start the engine. And then, as the MG responded to the gas pedal, he watched the fading of the pastoral scene, the windshield framing a changing picture. He caught one final glimpse of moonlit water and serene meadowland. The car turned onto Wharf Street and he saw the rough cobblestones that smothered all the flowers. He saw the jagged splintered outlines of piers and warehouses. The car was approaching Vernon and now he could see the shacks and the tenements. He began to hear the night noises of Vernon Street, the yowling of alley cats, the barking of mongrels, the dismal drumming moaning sound that came from hundreds of overcrowded rooms.

"Slow down," he said.

She looked at him. "Should I stop the car?"

"I didn't say that. Just slow down."

The car slackened speed. He sat stiffly, staring

straight ahead. She kept giving him side glances.

Finally she murmured, "What's the matter?"

"Nothing," he said.

In the distance there was the clattering screech of domestic discord. From some third-floor flat the cracked soprano of a fishwife's voice was a saw-toothed blade, while the rumbled oaths of the drunken husband were aimed past the woman, past the roof, going up to the sky.

And yet Kerrigan felt envious. The fishwife and her man would wind up in bed hugging each other. They'd stay together because they belonged together. They both came from the same roots, Vernon cradles.

He heard the calm voice of Loretta Channing the voice of a stranger asking for directions. He scarcely heard his own reply. As he told her to make a turn on Vernon, a chorus of Vernon voices came to him with the sullen query, what's she doing down here if she don't know her way around.

On Vernon Street the car was moving very slowly. A stumbling drunk lurched into the path of the car, was missed by inches, and shouted some dirty words to the driver. The words were very dirty and she winced. Kerrigan looked back and recognized the man. It was his next-door neighbor.

She put more pressure on the gas pedal. The MG leaped away from the flood of obscenity.

She said, "I'm glad we got away from that."

He told himself to keep his mouth shut.

At Third and Vernon he told her to make a right turn and they went down Third going past the street lamps, and toward the middle of the block he told her to stop the car. She looked at him questioningly. He pointed to a two-storied wooden dwelling that had a cardboard placard in its front window. The glow from the nearest street lamp showed two words scrawled in crayon on the placard. One word was in Greek letters. Under it was the same word in English – "Marriages."

He motioned her out of the car. Then together they stood at the front door and he rapped his knuckles on the wood. There were no lights in the house and he had to rap for several minutes before the door opened. The old Greek stood there, wearing a tattered bathrobe, needing a shave, his eyes clouded with interrupted slumber.

"You got a license handy?" Kerrigan asked.

The Greek blinked once. Then he was fully awake. "Plenty of licenses," he said. "I always have licenses."

He was a small man in his middle seventies. His head was bald except for three little bushes of white hair, one above each ear and one in the center. He smiled and showed a toothless mouth. He said, "The ring. You have the ring?"

Kerrigan shook his head. He looked at Loretta. Her face was calm and she was gazing past the old Greek and breathing quietly and not saying anything.

The Greek said, "I'll find a ring somewhere."

He beckoned them into the house. In the small and shabby parlor he switched on a lamp, then went into another room. Loretta sat down on a flimsy chair. Kerrigan stood in the middle of the floor, not looking at her. His legs felt heavy, as though weighted with lead.

A few minutes passed, and then the Greek came into the parlor carrying a bottle of ink and a pen and a large sheet of white paper rolled up, fastened with a rubber band. He took off the rubber band and put the paper in Kerrigan's hand. Kerrigan stared at the scrolled border and the printed words that told him he was looking at a marriage license. He swallowed very hard, and then he walked to the chair in which Loretta was seated and he said, "You sign it first."

Loretta looked at the Greek. "Is this paper a legitimate document?"

The old man nodded emphatically. "It comes from City Hall. My son works in the Marriage Bureau. Tomorrow he takes it back and puts it in the file."

She said quietly, "I want to be sure this is legal."

Kerrigan frowned. "Sure it's legal," he said. "Look at the printing on it."

The Greek said, "Nothing to worry about. I make real marriages. For many years I do this work. Never any trouble."

"If it isn't legal," Loretta murmured, "it's worthless, it doesn't mean anything."

The Greek twitched his lips and looked up at the ceiling. Then he glared at Loretta and said loudly, "This is genuine marriage license. I tell you it goes into the files."

Loretta got up from the chair and walked to the small table where the Greek had placed the pen and the ink. She picked up the pen, dipped it in the ink bottle, and then for a long moment she stared at Kerrigan. His head was lowered and he was gazing at the carpet. Loretta took a deep breath and signed her name to the license and then she handed the pen to Kerrigan.

He moved slowly toward the table. The pen vibrated in his trembling hand. He knew she was watching him and he tried to keep his hand from trembling. The trembling became worse and he couldn't move the pen toward the paper.

He heard her saying, "What are you waiting for?"

There was no way to answer that.

"Just sign your name," she said. "That's all you have to do. Put your name on the dotted line."

He stood there gaping at the paper that had her name written on it, with the dotted line waiting for his name.

Then he heard the Greek saying, "Maybe this man cannot write. Many men they come here and they cannot write their name."

"I can write," Kerrigan mumbled. As he spoke, he could feel the perspiration dripping from his forehead.

"What is happening?" the Greek asked quietly and seriously. "Why you not sign the paper?"

"Don't hurry him," Loretta said. "Let him pull himself together."

"He looks nervous," the Greek said. "I think he is very nervous."

"Really?" Her tone was musing. "I'd say that's rather strange. After all, this was his idea."

"Maybe he changes his mind." The old man spoke solemnly. "After all, marriage is no joke. It is a big step. Many men, they get scared."

"Well," she said, "if he wants to back out, this is the time to do it."

Kerrigan turned slowly and looked at her. She was smiling at him. He pivoted hard, bent over the table, and signed his name to the marriage license.

Then he picked up the license, shoved it at the old man, and said, "All right, let's get this over with. Where's the ring?"

The Greek put his hand in a pocket of the bathrobe, groped in there for a moment, and then took out a nickel-plated ring. It was thick and had a hinge that allowed it

to open and close. Kerrigan took a closer look and saw it
was a ring from a loose-leaf notebook.

"For God's sake," he said. "This ain't no wedding ring."

The old man shrugged. "It was all I could find." He
looked at Loretta and said, "Later he gets you a better
ring. This one here is only for the ceremony."

He handed the ring to Kerrigan. Then he opened a
drawer of the table and took out a Bible. As he leafed
through the pages, he said, "The price for the ceremony
is two dollars and fifty-two cents. That is total price. Two
dollars for performing marriage. Fifty cents for license.
You will please pay in advance."

Kerrigan frowned. "What's the two cents for?"

"I charge two cents for ring," the old man said. He
kept his eyes on the printed text while extending his
palm for the money. Then the money was in his hand
and he averted his eyes from the Bible just long enough
to count the cash. He put the bills and silver in the
pocket of his bathrobe, took a firmer grip on the Bible,
and said, "Now the bride will stand next to the groom."

It was three hours later and Kerrigan had his head
buried in a pillow. His eyes were shut tightly but he
wasn't asleep. He was trying to grope his way through
the fog of an alcoholic stupor. It was apparent to him
that he'd consumed an excessive amount of whisky, and
now his brain was crammed with a lot of little discs that
wouldn't stop spinning. His skull felt as though it were
swollen to many times its normal size. He told himself
he was really in sad shape, and wondered how in hell
he'd fallen into this condition.

He begged his mind to start working, to give him some
information concerning tonight's events, but his thoughts
stumbled along a tricky path leading nowhere.

Then gradually the fog cleared just a little, the discs slowed down, and he realized he was coming out of it. As his brain went into gear, he kept his eyes shut, telling himself not to think about now, not even to take a look and see where he was. What he had to do was straighten the track and follow it very slowly and carefully and bring it up to now.

On the wall of his closed eyelids a light showed and then widened and it became a series of pictures that told him what had happened. He saw himself placing the ring on her finger. Then sound came into it and he heard the old man saying, "I now pronounce you husband and wife." And then the old man was telling him to kiss her. She stood there smiling at him and waiting to be kissed. The old man said, "Go on, kiss her." He glared at the old man and growled, "Goddamnit, mind your own business." He heard her saying to the old man, "Please forgive my husband. I think he's upset about something."

The picture continued. He saw himself walking out of the old Greek's house, and heard her footsteps following. He turned and looked at her and said, "Where d'ya wanna go?" She shrugged and murmured, "It's up to you." He said loudly, "I guess we ought to celebrate." She shrugged again, smiling pleasantly and saying, "Anything you say, dear." And then the smile faded as she said, "You look as if you need a drink."

He closed his eyes and saw more pictures. They were in the car and she had it headed down Third Street, then coming up Fourth and arriving on Vernon. She said, "You really need a drink, I know you do." And then the MG was parked outside Dugan's Den and they were entering the taproom. The place was empty now and Dugan was getting ready to close up for the night. Loretta put some

money in Dugan's hand and Dugan put a bottle on the
bar. She poured the whisky into the jiggers. Then she
lifted the glass and proposed a toast. "Here's to our
wedding night," she said. He lifted his glass, gazed
moodily at the amber liquor, then shot it down his throat.
Again she tilted the bottle and filled the jiggers. She said,
"Another toast. Here's to my husband." He looked at her
and muttered, "Let's get out of here. I don't feel like
drinking." But a moment later he had the glass to his
lips and then he was waiting for it to be filled again.

Then the picture got hazy. They stood there at the bar,
and the glasses were filled and emptied and filled again.
It went on and on like that, and then they were walking
out of Dugan's Den. Or rather, she was trying to keep
him on his feet while he staggered toward the door. Then
she helped him into the car and said, "Now you're really
drunk." His head was down and he tried to lift it to look
at her. But he couldn't. And he couldn't say anything.

The pictures were fading away but he managed to get
a vague impression of the car coming to a stop, the
weaving and stumbling as she helped him up some steps
and through a doorway. He didn't know what room he
was in now. For just the fraction of an instant he caught
a flash of Loretta sitting on a sofa and watching him as
he staggered across a room. Then everything was black
and it stayed black. He buried his head deeper in the
pillow and thought, The hell with it, in the morning
you'll find out where you are. But then he felt the hand
on his thigh.

My God, he thought, she's in the bed with me.

He tried to pull way from the hand. An arm circled
his middle and drew him closer to the warm softness of
a woman.

"Come on," the woman said. Her voice was languid. "Come on," she said sleepily.

Again he tried to pull away. But now her grip was tighter.

"You hear me?" Her voice was louder. "I said come on."

"No," he mumbled. "Let go of me."

"What? What's that?"

"You hear me. Just keep away. Go back to sleep."

"You kidding?"

"I'm telling you to let go. Stay on your side of the bed."

"Are you talking to me?" Her tone was incredulous. "What's wrong with you? Why do you have your clothes on?"

He frowned. Either her voice had changed or his drunkenness caused him to think it was someone else's voice.

Or maybe it really was someone else's voice.

His head moved on the pillow, and very slowly he turned over so that he could look at her face. While he turned, his eyes were wide open, and he saw the dark wall, the moonlit ceiling, then the window that showed the moon far out there. The moon was like a big spotlight that seemed to be focused on himself and his companion.

He was staring at her.

It was his stepmother.

Their eyes were only inches apart and they were gaping at each other as though they couldn't believe what they saw. Lola had her mouth opened as wide as she could get it. Her lungs made a dragging sound as she gasped for air.

Kerrigan groaned without sound. He seriously pondered the problem of how to become invisible.

For a long moment neither of them could move. They

just went on gaping at each other. Then all at once Lola gave him a violent push that hurled him off the edge of the bed. He landed on the floor with a heavy thud. For purely practical reasons he decided to stay there for the time being. He stayed there and listened to the sound of the bedsprings as Lola's ponderous weight came off the mattress, then rapid and frantic sounds as she moved around and tried to find something to cover her.

The sounds went on as he sat there on the floor and groaned and sighed and pressed his hands to his head. He heard the noise of the closet door, the rustling of fabrics as clothes were pulled from hangers. He was half sobered now, and he began to consider the feasibility of a fast exit from the room.

But before he could arrive at a decision, there was the click of a wall switch and the room was brightly lit. He blinked several times and then he looked up and saw the big woman who stood there wearing a nightgown. She had her hands on her hips, her eyes a pair of seething caldrons.

"What is this?" she demanded. "What the hell goes on here?"

He choked, gulped hard, choked again, then blurted, "It's nothing, I just made a mistake."

As he said it, he realized how stupid and crazy it sounded. He blinked again, gazing blankly at the face of his stepmother. But she was looking at the empty bed, focusing on the pillow that should have shown her husband's face but showed only a question mark.

"Where is he?" she asked loudly. "Where's your father?"

Kerrigan lifted himself from the floor. He sat down on the edge of the bed, his head in his hands. He made a vague guess as to where his father was. Chances were that Tom was in the house of Rita Montanez.

Lola said, "He claimed he hadda go to the bathroom." Her eyes narrowed. "I'm gonna have a look," she muttered grimly, "and he'd better be in there."

She went out of the room. Kerrigan groped through the haze of his drunkenness and told himself to make a rapid trip to Rita's house and drag Tom out of there. But as he lifted himself from the bed, the floor seemed to slant and he had trouble staying on his feet.

And as he moved toward the door, the whisky in his veins made it several doors instead of one. He was still trying to find the right door when Lola re-entered the room.

"He ain't in the bathroom," she announced through tightened lips. She glared at Kerrigan. She said accusingly, "What are you and him up to?"

He sat down very slowly and carefully on a chair that wasn't there. Again he was on the floor, wondering what had happened to the chair.

Lola studied him for a long moment. "How many quarts did you drink?"

He shrugged kind of sadly. "I didn't have much. Guess I can't hold it."

"The hell you can't. From the looks of you, you're holding a gallon."

She took hold of his wrists, pulled him up from the floor, and put him in the chair that he hadn't been able to find. "Now then," she said, "I want some information. Where is he?"

Kerrigan stared dumbly at Tom's wife and said, "Maybe he went for a walk."

"At this time of night? Where would he walk?"

The whisky fog came drifting in. Kerrigan blinked several times and said, "Maybe he got lost." He gazed longingly at the bed and thought how pleasant it would be to go back to sleep.

Lola studied him once more and saw he was in no condition to give sensible answers. She gestured disgustedly and turned her back to him.

Suddenly she snapped her fingers. Then her head turned from side to side as she made a hasty examination of the room.

"Sure enough," she said. "His clothes ain't here."

She started to take deep breaths. Lola was about to lose her temper on a grand scale.

Despite his drunkenness, he managed to say, "No use getting sore about it. After all, it's a helluva hot night. Maybe he went out for a bottle of beer. To cool himself off."

"I'll cool him off," Lola said. "I'll break his goddamn neck, that's what I'll do."

She started to move around the room, searching for a suitable weapon. Kerrigan winced as he saw her lifting a thick glass ash tray, hefting it in her hand to test the weight of it. Apparently it wasn't heavy enough. She slammed it to the floor, then darted to the open closet and reached in and pulled out a long-handled scrubbing brush. The business end of the brush was an inch of bristles and a two-inch thickness of wood.

Lola had a firm grip on the handle of the brush. She held it with both hands, aiming it at empty air and taking a few practice swipes. Then, wanting a better target, she looked around for something solid. Kerrigan heard footsteps in the hall and he thought, It's gonna be crowded in here.

The door opened and Tom walked in. An instant later there was a loud whacking noise and Tom yelled, "Ouch!" Then there was more whacking, more yelling, and considerable activity. Tom was trying to run in several directions at once. He collided with Kerrigan, bounced away, staggered sideways, and received a wallop from Lola that spun him around like a punching bag. He tried to crawl under the bed, but there wasn't enough space between the springs and the floor. He was much too bulky to squeeze through. The flat side of the brush landed on him and in a frenzied effort to get away from the blows he gave a mighty heave with his shoulders, so that the bed was raised on two legs. He heaved again and the bed fell over on its side. Lola kept swinging the brush and Tom was asking her to wait just a minute so they could talk it over. Lola's reply was another whack. The sound resembled a pistol shot. Tom looked at Kerrigan and shouted, "For God's sake, make her stop."

Kerrigan shrugged, as though to say there was no way to stop Lola once she got started. He grinned stupidly, drunkenly, and then he started toward the door. But again it was several doors, and it seemed as if the ceiling were coming down. He couldn't stay on his legs. The floor came up and he was flat on his face. The dazed grin remained on his lips as he heard the continued uproar. Somehow the noise of the violence was softened in his whisky-drenched brain. It was strangely soothing, almost like a lullaby. For a hazy instant he tried to understand it. But the feeling was so pleasant, so comforting, it told him to fall asleep, just fall asleep. And as the blackness enveloped him, he sensed there was nothing strange about it, after all. It was merely the sound of the house where he lived. It was as though he'd been away and he'd come back, and it was nice to be home again.

CHAPTER 13

In the darkness of the alcoholic sleep, he drifted through
a glass-lined canal that had the labels of whisky bottles
on its walls. The labels were varicolored and there were
too many colors floating past his eyes. He told himself to
stop looking at the labels, he'd soon be getting a head-
ache. But then the glass became wood and there was no
canal at all, just a dark alley and some moonlight showing the sides of the wooden shacks. He followed the path
of the moonlight as it flowed onto the rutted paving and
he saw the dried bloodstains.

"Goddamn it," he said, waking up.

He could feel a pillow under his head, and he heard
someone breathing beside him. Before he looked to see
who it was, he sat up, groaning and holding his head
and wishing he had an ice bag. He blinked hard several
times, and suddenly his eyes were wide as he realized
this was Bella's room.

His head turned slowly. He looked at Bella. She was
sound asleep, resting on her side. It was very hot and
sticky in the room and she wasn't wearing anything.

The window showed the dark gray-pink of early morning. On the dresser the hands of the alarm clock pointed
to four-forty-five. He told himself to get out of bed and
go into his own room. Looking down at himself, he saw
that he was wearing only a pair of shorts. He glanced
across the floor, searching for his clothes, and saw shirt

and jacket and trousers draped carelessly over a chair, Bella's dress on top of the heap.

Moving carefully, trying not to make any noise, he climbed out of bed and headed toward the chair. It seemed as if a ton of rocks was pressing down on him and crushing his skull. As he reached for his clothes, he stumbled forward, hit the chair, knocked it over, and went down with it.

He cursed without sound, getting up very slowly. Then he had his shoes in one hand, his shirt in the other, the jacket and trousers dangling from his arm as he walked unsteadily toward the door.

He was only a step away from the door when he heard Bella's voice. "Just where d'ya think you're going?"

"I got my own bed."

"Yeah?"

"Yeah," he said. He groped for the door handle. His hand closed on it.

"Listen, louse," Bella said. She was off the bed and coming toward him. She gave him a shove that sent him away from the door. She pointed to the bed and said, "Get back in there."

"You talkin' to me?"

She put her weight on one leg and clapped a hand to her hip. Then, shifting slightly, so that she blocked his path to the door, she said, "You might as well make yourself comfortable. We're gonna have a discussion."

"Not now," he said.

"Right now." Her eyes dared him to make a move toward the door. "We're gonna have it out here and now."

"For God's sake." He pointed to the alarm clock. "Look what time it is. I gotta get some sleep. Gotta get rid of this hangover."

"That's what I want to talk about," she said. "How come you got drunk last night?"

He didn't reply. He dropped the shoes to the floor, flipped the clothes aside, and walked slowly to the bed. As he sat down on the edge of the mattress, his hands were pressed tightly to his temples, as though trying to squeeze the whisky fog from his brain.

Bella came around the side of the bed and stood facing him. "I know you're not a drinker," she said. "You musta had a reason for getting drunk. Come on, let's have it. What happened last night?"

"Nothing."

"I'll bet." She snorted. And then, her eyes narrowed, "I found you stretched out in the hall outside Lola's room. You were stiff as a board."

"So what?"

"So it made me curious. You wouldn't get loaded like that unless you had something on your mind. Something you couldn't handle."

He looked at her. "What gives you that idea?"

"I just know, that's all. I know you."

His eyes were dull, gazing past her. "You think you know me."

She stood there studying his face. She said, "I took the trouble to drag you in here and take your clothes off and put you in bed."

"Thanks," he said sourly. "Thanks a lot."

"I didn't do it for thanks. I did it so I'd be around when you come out of it. We got some things to talk about. I wanna know the score on this. I got a right to know."

He frowned at her. "You got one hell of a crust, that's what you got. I didn't ask you to put me in this room."

"It ain't the first time you been here. You been in this

room a lotta times. More times than I can count. And I never dragged you in, either. You always come in on your own two feet."

He took a deep breath. He started to get up from the bed and she pushed him back. She did it roughly and he bounced on the mattress. He made another attempt to get up and she pushed him again, harder this time. His head went back against the pillow. It felt like iron banging his skull. He told himself to close his eyes and go to sleep. His benumbed brain said, Forget about her, forget about everything, just go to sleep.

But then she was leaning over him, shaking him. She said, "Come on, come out of it."

"Goddamnit, leave me alone."

He shut his eyes tightly and tried to roll over on his side but she pulled at his shoulder and wouldn't let him do it. He mumbled an oath and reached out blindly to shove her away, and as his hand made contact with Bella, a current passed through him from her to him, from him to her, and he was aching to hold on, hold her tighter, pull her to him and find her lips and taste her mouth. But just then he heard the soundless voice that said, No.

It was a blast of icy realization that sliced through the heat of his senses and the thick mist of the hangover. He moved spasmodically to the other side of the bed, then sat up stiffly, staring at her. Ice was in his eyes as he said, "Keep away from me."

She sat there on the other side of the bed. She didn't say anything. She just looked at him.

He said, "And put something on."

She smiled thinly. "Does it bother you?"

He clamped his lips tightly. He turned his head so he wouldn't see her.

Her voice was a light jab, flicking at him. "It excites you, don't it? You don't want it to excite you."

"Listen, Bella—"

"Yes?"

But he couldn't take it from there. He swallowed hard. She said, "Well, go on. I'm listening."

He told himself he'd have to say it sooner or later. He might as well say it now and get it over with. For a moment his eyes were closed and he was trying to find the words. And then, gazing straight ahead and seeing the wall on the other side of the room, he said, "It's all finished. We gotta call it quits."

He waited for her to say something.

Long moments passed. There was no sound in the room.

He went on gazing at the opposite wall. Finally he said, "Last night I got married."

"You what?"

"Got married."

"You joking?"

"No."

There was another long pause. When she spoke again, her voice sounded queer, sort of strangled. "Where'd you pull this caper?"

"At the Greek's place," he said. He spoke tonelessly. "Bought a license. She signed her name to it. I signed my name. I put a ring on her finger."

"That girl I seen you with? That floozie from uptown?"

"Yeah." He sighed heavily. He wondered if there was anything else to say.

He heard Bella saying, "Tell me how it happened."

"It happened, that's all. It just happened."

"You know what you're saying?"

He nodded again.

Bella said, "Maybe I'm crazy. Maybe I'm hearing things." She stood up. She sat down. She stood up again. She began to walk back and forth along the length of the bed. Finally she stopped, and with both hands she gripped the bedpost, as though to steady herself. Then, biting her lip, her eyes shut tightly, she made a sound as though she were feeling intense physical pain.

He rubbed his knuckles across his brow. He wondered what caused him to stay in this room when there was every reason to walk out.

"Can't believe it," Bella said aloud to herself. "It just ain't possible." And then her tone changed, there was pleading in her voice. "Didja know what you were doing? You couldn't have known. After all, you were drunk."

"No," he said gruffly. "I got drunk later."

"With her?"

"Yeah," he said. "We were celebrating."

"Where?" Her hands tightened on the bedpost.

"What difference does it make?"

"I'm askin' you something. Where'd you do the celebrating? Was it in a hotel room?"

He shook his head. Again he gave a heavy sigh. He said, "We went to Dugan's Den."

"Then where'd you go?"

His jaw hardened. "All right," he muttered, "let's drop the questions."

"You'll sit there and answer them. You'll tell me where you went after you left Dugan's Den."

He turned and frowned at her. "What're you getting at?"

She wasn't looking at him. Her voice was a grinding whisper. "You know what I'm getting at. You've told me about the license and the ring. And the celebration. Now I want to hear the rest of it. I want to know all about the wedding night."

He aimed the frown at the floor. "We didn't do anything, if that's what you mean."

She let go of the bedpost. She breathed in and out and it was almost like a sigh of relief. The corners of her mouth moved up just a trifle, starting to build a smile.

Kerrigan went on frowning. He heard himself saying, "The way it happened, we walked out of Dugan's and she had her car parked outside and we climbed in. She drove me back here and she helped me into the house. Then she was sitting on the sofa and I was moving around, I didn't know where the hell I was going. Went down the hall and got the rooms mixed up and landed in the wrong bed."

"You weren't as mixed up as you thought you were," Bella said. She had the smile fully glowing in her eyes. "You were on your way to the right bed. You're in it now."

He stared at her. She was moving toward him, coming slowly across the room. He told himself to get up but somehow he couldn't lift his limbs. As he watched Bella approaching, it was like a wall closing in on him.

She was saying, "Don't you see the way it is? Last night was just a joke, it wasn't for real, and you know it. Whatever it was that made you do it, we'll check that off, it ain't important. Only one thing matters. You're here with me."

"No," he said. "No."

Her smile widened and brightened and she said, "You don't mean that. You mean yes."

"Now wait." And his hand was lifted, telling her to stay away.

She flung herself at him, wrapping her arms around his middle. He fell back with her weight pressing against him. Her eyes were wild and her lips found his mouth and he could feel the flame rising in his body, the red-black flame that curled and swept in wide arcs, and he held her tightly, his heart pounding. But just then he heard the soundless voice of his brain saying, You damn fool, you're falling into a trap, get out, get out.

He tried to push her away. She wouldn't let go of him. He seized her wrists and twisted hard, then gave her a violent shove that sent her to the floor. He stood up quickly, lunged across the room, and picked up his shoes and the shirt and the jacket and trousers. He started toward the door. Then abruptly he came to a stop. He glared at her. He said, "I oughta push your face in for trying a trick like that."

It seemed she was speaking to the bed. "Well, I tried."

"Damn right you did. And you saw what it got you. You're lucky it didn't get you a broken jaw."

She looked at him. "I'm still here, if you feel like slugging me."

"It ain't worth the effort," he said. Then he braced himself, expecting that she'd leap at him with clawing fingernails.

For some moments she didn't move. Then very slowly she got up from the floor. She walked across the room, picked up a robe, and put it on. He watched her as she reached into a pocket, took out a pack of cigarettes and a book of matches. Her voice was oddly matter of fact as she said, "Want one?"

He shook his head. Her eyes were blank, puzzled.

She was lighting a cigarette. "You sure you don't want one?"

He breathed hard. "Only thing I want from you is a definite understanding. From here on in you're gonna leave me alone. You'll hafta get it through your head I'm a married man."

"By the way," she murmured casually, "where is she?"

He blinked a few times.

She took a slow easy drag at the cigarette. "Well?" She watched the smoke drifting away from her lips. "Come on, tell me. Where's the bride?"

His mouth was opened loosely. He went on blinking.

"I'll tell you where she is," Bella said. "She's sound asleep in a nice clean bed. In a nice clean house. In a nice respectable neighborhood."

He swallowed hard. He couldn't say anything.

Bella said, "It stands to reason she wouldn't stay here. She'd be a damn fool to spend the night in this dump."

"All right," he muttered. "That's enough."

Bella looked at the cigarette held loosely in her fingers. She spoke to the cigarette. "Sure, the bride took a run-out. And who can blame her? The groom brings her to a house with the plaster chipping off the walls and the furniture coming apart and empty beer bottles all over the floor. It's a wonder she let herself sit on the sofa. This afternoon she'll be taking her dress to the cleaners, you can bet on that and your money's safe. Another thing she'll do, she'll go to the beauty parlor and have her hair washed, an extra soaping just to make sure. After all, in these Vernon rat traps you never know, you can pick up anything. What she really oughta do is spray herself with DDT."

"Shut up," he said. "You better shut up."

Bella shrugged. "Well, anyway, she's breathing easier now. That cleaner, fresher air uptown."

He stood motionless. The quiet in the room was un-
bearable, and he knew he had to say something. His
mouth was tight as he said, "You don't get the point. All
she did was walk out of the house. She didn't walk out
on me."

"That ain't what I'm saying." Bella spoke very quietly.
But now the cigarette trembled in her fingers. "Cantcha
see what I'm trying to tell ya? No matter how much she
wants you, she can't get away from uptown. And sure as
hell you can't get away from here."

"Can't I?" His eyes aimed past Bella, seeing past the
walls, past Vernon rooftops and sky. "All it takes is streetcar fare. Just a matter of fifteen cents."

The cigarette split in half. The lighted end hit the floor
and scorched the carpet. Bella stepped on the burning
stub. She looked at the scattered ashes. She was sobbing
without sound as she said, "Don't throw your money
away. It's a dime and a nickel wasted. All you'll be doing
is taking yourself for a ride."

"It's gonna be more than that," he said. "I'll be going
somewhere." And then, as though Bella weren't in the
room, he said softly to himself, "She's there, she's waiting
for me."

"You fool," Bella whispered. "You poor fool."

He looked at her. There was a practical tone in his
voice as he said, "I'm leaving tonight. As soon as I get
home from work. Tell Lola not to cook for me. I'm gonna
be in a hurry."

Bella nodded very slowly. She gazed vacantly at the
door behind him. Her lips moved automatically. "All
right, I'll tell her not to cook for you."

He turned away from her. He opened the door and
walked out of the room.

Then in his own room he was putting on his work clothes. He was thinking, Tomorrow morning it'll be a different room, a different house, a different street. From now on everything's gonna be different, gonna be better. His brain could taste the pleasant flavor of saying goodby to all Vernon dwellings, all Vernon faces.

There was a sound from the bed where Frank was sleeping fitfully. Turning over on his side, Frank grunted and let out a dry cough. Frank's face was toward the window, and as the morning light hit him, he opened his eyes. He saw Kerrigan sitting in a chair near the window. Kerrigan had just finished tying a shoelace and he was sitting up straight.

Frank's eyes were shiny. His mouth began to twitch. He lifted his head from the pillow, bracing himself on his elbows. He said, "Quit watching me."

Kerrigan made a gesture of weary annoyance. "Go back to sleep."

"Why d'ya keep watching me?"

"For God's sake, come off that routine."

"I can't come off," Frank said. "You keep me on it. You won't leave me alone."

Kerrigan shrugged. It was no use going on with it.

"I'm warning you," Frank said. "You better stop watching me."

He told himself to go easy. He said softly, "All right, let's skip it. I got other things on my mind."

"Like what?"

He smiled amiably at his brother. "Well, I finally went and did it. I got hitched."

Frank blinked a few times. "For real?"

He nodded. "License and ring and the whole works. Last night at the Greek's."

Frank lowered his legs off the side of the bed. He leaned forward stiffly, his skinny torso slanted like something activated by a lever. His voice was dull and metallic as he said, "Who is she?"

"You don't know her."

"Maybe I do," Frank said. "What's her name?"

"Loretta."

"The blonde?"

Kerrigan flinched. He had an odd feeling, as though he were bolted to the chair.

"The blonde with green eyes?" Frank asked. "The tasty dish from uptown?"

He sat there and stared at Frank.

"Sure," Frank said. "I know her."

"What do you mean, you know her?"

Frank parted his lips, his mouth curled up at the corners, revealing his yellow teeth. He didn't say anything.

Kerrigan tried to get up from the chair. He couldn't move. He said very slowly, "Whatever's on your mind, don't hold it back. Let's have it."

The toothy grimace stayed on Frank's face. He was looking past Kerrigan and saying, "I've seen her in Dugan's Den. Seen her there a lotta times. One night she bought me a drink. We talked. We stood there at the bar and she bought me more drinks and we talked."

"What about?"

"I don't remember," Frank said. The grimace widened. "All I remember is looking at her and thinking she reminded me of someone."

"Who?" It was blurted, almost a shout.

But Frank didn't seem to hear. "It wasn't the face or the body. It wasn't the eyes, either. More like the feeling you get when you're in a room that looks different but somehow you know you've been there before. Can't put your finger on what it is, but you know it just the same. That's what I remember mostly, that feeling. It was sorta weird, it gimme the chills. But that don't matter. I like to get the chills. It feels nice when I start to shiver. So there we stood at the bar and I was shivering and it felt real nice. And then, when she walked out, I waited just long enough to say the alphabet from A to Q. Then I followed her."

"You did what?"

"Followed her," Frank said, speaking to the wall.

"Was she alone?"

Frank's head moved jerkily up and down. "She'd come to Dugan's to pick up her brother, the lush. But he wouldn't leave. He told her to go home alone. On the street I saw her walking toward that little car she drives. The little gray job with the wire wheels. It was parked on the other side of Vernon, halfway down the block. All the other spaces were taken up by trucks. So she hadda do some walking to get to the car. That gave me plenty of time to follow her. I was shivering real good then, nice and cold. She looked so slim and trim and neat, so clean and shining, like something you see in a dream. That's it. In a dream. And I'd been there before. The same moon. The same street. Everything the same except for one thing. Her name. It wasn't Loretta."

It seemed to Kerrigan that the walls were liquid, forming waves that rolled slowly toward him. He begged himself to get up from the chair and run out of the room. But he couldn't budge. He heard himself saying, "All right, you saw her walking to the car. Then what?"

"Nothing," Frank said. "She drove away in the car."

"You've pulled this stunt before? You've followed women down the street?"

Frank didn't answer.

"Tell me," Kerrigan said. He was up from the chair, moving toward the bed. He grabbed Frank's shoulders. "You're gonna tell me."

"Tell you what?" Frank uttered a soundless laugh. "Something you know already?"

He dropped his hands to his knees. He backed away from Frank, his eyes riveted to his brother's face. And yet his inner vision didn't show a face at all. It showed a dark alley, with the moonlight coming down and spraying brightly on dried bloodstains.

CHAPTER 14

He turned away from Frank, hurried out of the room, and walked out of the house. He was trying very hard not to think about Frank. He wished he could reach with his fingers into his mind and drag Frank out of there.

On Vernon Street, walking toward Wharf, he saw the row of wooden shacks off Vernon between Third and Fourth, and he thought, Maybe it was Mooney, after all, or maybe it was Nick Andros. He walked faster, seeing more wooden shacks and the shabby fronts of tenements and he muttered without sound, There's more than one creep lives in these dumps, more than one hophead and bay-rum drinker and all kinds of queers. It might have been any one of them and maybe you'll never know for sure who it was. He pleaded with himself to let it rest there, to bury it and forget about it. But his face was gray and his breathing was heavy and he was still thinking about Frank.

And hours later, hauling crates along Pier 17, he didn't feel the weight of heavy boxes tugging at his arms and pressing on his spine. The only pressure he felt was inside his head. He couldn't stop thinking about Frank.

At four in the afternoon the sky began to darken and the river took on a metallic sheen. Black clouds moved in and shadowed the piers and warehouses and the street that bordered the docks. At a few minutes past five, as some of the dock workers started to leave the piers and head for home, the air was split with thunder. Pier bosses and foremen shouted feverish commands. Then all at once it was coming down, and it hit with terrific force. It was like a lake falling from the sky.

The docks were deserted. And soon the streets were empty. There was no human activity at all. There were only the darkness and the rumble of thunder and the relentless cascade of rain. The river was choppy with white caps, and angry waves came smashing at the piers.

Cursing, drenched to the skin, Kerrigan huddled under the stingy roof of a loading platform. He tried the big door that led into the warehouse. But the door was locked, and all he could do was press his back against it and try to keep from getting wetter than he was already.

He looked out across a few yards of wooden pier, the planks giving way to a newer driveway of concrete. Through the wall of falling rain he saw the raging foam of the river, and he could feel the vibration of the pier as the waves crashed against its pilings. Muttering an oath, he told himself it was a northeaster, and that meant it was due to last for hours and hours, and maybe days. He decided to take his chances with a run for home, and he braced himself, preparing to leap off the platform and make a beeline toward Vernon.

Just then he heard a clicking sound behind him. Someone had unlocked the big door. He told himself he'd been seen through one of the windows and some kindhearted character was inviting him to come in and get dry.

He worked the door handle and pushed against the door, and the heavy bulk of it swung slowly inward. As he entered the warehouse, he saw there were no bulbs lit, and he frowned puzzledly as he groped his way forward. He shouted, "Anybody around?"

There was no answer. The only sound was the dull roar of the storm outside.

His frown deepened. He took a few more steps, bumped into a barrel, circled around it, and kept on going. Scarcely any light came through the partially opened door to the loading platform, and now he moved in almost total darkness.

He decided the door had been unlocked by some gin hound who'd come out of it just long enough to do him a favor, and then had returned to an alcoholic slumber.

His hand came in contact with the edge of a large box. He sat down on the box and wished he had a book of matches and a pack of cigarettes. For a few moments he played with the idea of getting the hell out of here. But the air in the warehouse was warm and somehow comfortable, and a lot drier than the weather outside. He figured he might as well sit here for a while.

But then, he thought, the storm would probably get worse and last for hours, and he was pretty hungry, getting hungrier all the time. And the problem of love had remained.

"The hell with this," he muttered aloud, and turned his head, looking for the column of gray light that would reveal the exit.

All he saw was blackness, and the dim gray rectangles of the small windows. The windows were high off the floor, and that was one thing. Another thing was the fact that they were made of wired glass and he'd have one mess of a time smashing his way through.

And yet he wasn't thinking much about that. He was concentrating on the door, telling himself he'd left the door open and now it was closed.

His mouth was set in a thin line as he thought,
Whoever let me in here is making sure I don't get out.

In that same moment, he heard footsteps.

The sounds came from behind him. He knew that if he
turned his head, he would see who it was. His eyes had
become accustomed to the darkness, and the windows
afforded just enough light for recognizing a face. But in
the instant that he told himself to turn and look, his
instinct contradicted the impulse and commanded him to
duck, to dodge, to evade an unseen weapon.

He threw himself sideways, falling off the box.
There was a whirring sound that sliced the air, and
then the crash of a thick club or something, landing
on the top of the box where he'd been seated. He was
on his knees, crouched at the side of the box, listening
intently for a sound that would give him his assailant's
position.

Again he heard footsteps, and the shuffling noises told
him he was dealing with more than one attacker.

His sense of caution gave way to a grim curiosity. He
raised his head above the edge of the box and saw the
men. There were two of them. The dim gray light from
the windows was barely sufficient for him to estimate
their size and study their features. The initial glimpse
told him he was facing serious trouble. This was a professional wrecking team, a couple of dock ruffians who
charged a set fee for breaking a man's jaw, a higher fee
for removing an ear or an eye. And if the customer was
willing to meet their price, they'd go all the way and use
the river to hide the traces of what had been done. Their
business reputation was excellent. There were never any
disappointed customers.

Kerrigan could see their wide shoulders, the thickness

of their arms and wrists. They carried wooden clubs, and they wore brass knuckles.

Now there was no sound from the other side of the box. They were taking their time about it, and it was as though they were sending him a silent message, telling him they had him where they wanted him, and they'd be willing to wait until he made a move.

He bit his lip, wondering what he could do. He glanced around at the floor, but it offered nothing, there was no sign of ammunition or weapon. He cursed without sound. Whatever these men were planning to do, whatever damage they had in mind, they'd sure as hell arranged it carefully. He knew they'd followed him from Pier 17, and the thunderstorm had aided them in their scheme to corner him. But storm or no storm, they'd have cornered him anyway. They'd have waited for a convenient moment and a convenient place. As matters stood, they had trailed him to the warehouse, had peered through a window to make sure it was deserted, and then they'd found an entrance. They'd watched him getting soaked out there in the rain, so from there on it was easy. They'd simply unlocked the door to let him know it was dry in here and he was welcome. It was a friendly favor and he ought to thank them. He ought to tell them how much he appreciated their kindness.

There were five feet of wooden box separating him from the big men and the thick clubs and the brass knuckles.

One of the men was grinning at him.

The other man, somewhat shorter and wider than his partner, leaned forward just a little and said, "You ready for it? You ready to take it?"

"He looks ready," the taller man said.

They spoke quietly, yet their voices were distinct against the rumbling of the storm outside. In the shadows their eyes were little points of yellow and green light, and there was the bright gleam of the brass knuckles, the glow reflected on the thick clubs of rounded wood.

And then there was something else, another glow that caused Kerrigan to glance downward. He saw the glimmer on the metal handle attached under the lid of the box.

The short wide man was saying, "Let's find out if he's ready."

"All right," the other man said. "Let's take him."

Kerrigan grabbed the handle and got a tight two-handed hold on it and with all the power in his body he heaved upward and forward, doing it very fast so that the box was raised and pushed in almost the same moment. It was just as heavy as it was large, and he heard the loud thud as it collided with the men. There was another thud and he knew that one of the men had been knocked down. He was still pushing at the box and he went on pushing until the box toppled over onto the fallen man. There was the sound of something being crushed and the fallen man was screaming and trying to wriggle out from under the box and not being able to do it.

The short wide man had leaped backward and seemed to be debating whether to aid his partner or make a lunge at Kerrigan. Before he had a chance to arrive at a decision, Kerrigan rushed at him, coming in low, sending a shoulder against his knees and taking him to the floor.

As they hit the floor the short man used his club on Kerrigan's ribs. Kerrigan let out a cry of animal pain, and the man hit him again in the same place. It sent white-hot fire through his middle, then more fire as he took another blow from the club. He rolled himself away and managed to evade a blow aimed at his skull. The man leaped at him, kicked him in the spot where he'd been clubbed, then tried to turn him over, sort of prodding him with a heavy foot to get him over on his back. In the next moment he was on his back and he looked up and saw that the club was raised once more. The short man wore a businesslike expression and was taking careful aim with his eyes focused on Kerrigan's pelvis.

Then the club came down. Kerrigan raised both legs and took the blow on his thigh. In the same instant he snatched at the club, missed and snatched again and missed again, and the club slammed against his arm. But now he didn't feel the pain and he was getting to his feet and not thinking about the club or the brass knuckles. He walked toward the short wide man and feinted with his left hand. As the club flashed downward, he pulled away from it, going sideways, then moving in very close and chopping his right hand to the man's jaw. The man staggered backward and dropped the club. Kerrigan kept moving in, hooked a left to the side of the head, and then hauled off and threw a roundhouse right that lifted the man off the floor and sent him sailing to land flat on his back.

Kerrigan kept moving in. The man was scrambling to his feet. Kerrigan kicked him in the head and that sent him down again. The man was gasping as Kerrigan kicked him once more. Kerrigan reached down and pulled him to his knees and smashed him in the mouth.

The man screamed. He made a desperate attempt to

flee. Headed for the door of the loading platform, he ran
through the narrow path lined with crates and barrels.
He found the door and opened it and leaped out upon
the rain-swept platform.

But in the next instant the man was on his knees with
Kerrigan on top of him. Kerrigan's eyes were calmer now.
He was thinking in purely practical terms, knowing
there was only one way to deal with these professional
manglers. He thought, knock him out, then make him
talk.

He had one arm circling the man's throat. His other
arm was drawn back and then he let go with a kidney
punch that caused the man to scream again. Then
another kidney punch, and the force of it was enough to
take the two of them off the loading platform and onto
the planks of the pier. As they landed, the man made
a frantic effort to break loose, pumping his elbow into
Kerrigan's stomach. Kerrigan groaned and fell back
and saw the man running past the planks and onto the
concrete driveway that bordered the edge of the pier.

But there was too much rain, it was coming down too
hard, and the man could scarcely see where he was
going. The concrete driveway was a foggy, slippery path,
made treacherous by the foam coming up from the big
waves crashing against the pier. The man had taken only
a few steps when he lost his footing. Kerrigan was up
very fast, lunging at him and trying to grab him before
he went over the edge. There wasn't enough time for
that. The man went over and down and made a splash.
The raging current caught him and carried him away
and swallowed him.

Kerrigan walked back to the loading platform and
went inside the warehouse. He moved very slowly,

wearily, grimacing as he felt the hammering pain in his ribs and stomach. He went on leaden feet toward the spot where the other man was still trying to squirm out from under the heavy box.

"God in heaven," the man groaned. "Get this thing off me."

Kerrigan smiled dimly. "What's the hurry?"

"It's mashin' my chest. I can't hardly breathe."

"You're breathing all right. And you're talking. That's all we need for now."

The man had one arm free and he raised his hand to his eyes and let out a moan.

Kerrigan knelt at the side of the man. He took a close look at the man's face and saw there wasn't much color. The man's eyes were glazed and the lips were quivering with pain and supplication. He told himself that maybe the man's chest was crushed, that maybe the man would die. He decided he didn't give a damn.

He said, "Who hired you?"

The man's reply was another moan.

"If you won't talk," Kerrigan said, "you'll stay there under the box."

He stood up. He turned away from the moans of the crushed man. Facing the opened doorway of the loading platform, he listened to the sound of the rainstorm. It seemed to merge with the noise of a cyclone that whirled through his brain.

Just then he heard the man saying, "It was a woman."

And after that it seemed there was no sound at all. Just a frozen stillness. Again he turned very slowly, and he was looking down at the man.

"A woman," the man said. He moaned once more, and coughed a few times. He wheezed, "She lives on

Vernon Street. I think they call her Bella."

"Bella." He said it aloud to himself. Then he reached down and lifted the heavy box off the chest of the man. He heard the man's sigh of relief, the dragging sound of air pulled into tortured lungs.

The man rolled over on his side. He tried to get to his feet. He made it to his knees, shook his head slowly, and muttered, "This ain't no good. I'm in bad shape. You might as well call the Heat. At least they'll take me to a hospital."

"You don't need a hospital," Kerrigan said. He put his hands under the man's armpits, then used his arms as a hook to raise him from the floor.

The man leaned heavily against him and said, "Where's my partner?"

"In the river," Kerrigan said.

The man forgot his own pain and weakness. He stepped away from Kerrigan, his eyes dulled with a kind of brute sorrow. Then he shook his head slowly and said, "It just don't pay to take these jobs. They're not worth the grief. I'm all banged up inside and he's food for the fishes. All for a lousy twenty bucks."

"Is that what she paid you?"

The man nodded.

Kerrigan's eyes narrowed. "She pay in advance?"

"Yeah." The man put his hand against his trousers pocket.

"Let's have it," Kerrigan said.

It was two fives and a ten. The man handed him the bills and he folded them carefully. He said, "You sure she didn't give you more?"

The man tried to smile. "If she wanted you rubbed out complete, it would have cost her a hundred. For this

kind of job, to put a man outta action, we never charge
more than twenty."

"Bargain rates," Kerrigan muttered.

It was quiet for some moments. And then the man was
saying, "Look, mister, I got a record. I'm out on parole.
Wanna gimme a break?"

Kerrigan smiled dryly. "O.K.," he said. He pointed to
the doorway.

"Thanks," the man said. "Thanks a lot, mister."

Kerrigan watched him as he walked away, moving
slowly and painfully, pausing in the doorway to offer
a final gesture of gratitude, then limping out upon the
loading platform and vanishing in the storm.

Kerrigan looked down at the money folded in his hand.

CHAPTER 15

Despite his anxiety for a showdown with Bella, he pur-
posely delayed going home. For one thing, he wanted to
be very calm when he faced her. Also, and more important, he wanted the discussion to be strictly private. On
Wharf Street he entered a diner, ordered a heavy meal,
took a few bites and pushed the plate aside. He sat there
ordering countless cups of coffee and filling the ash tray
with cigarette stubs. Then later he walked along Wharf
through the storm, found a thirty-cent movie house, and
bought a ticket.

When he came out of the movie it was past midnight.
The storm had slackened and now the rainfall was a
steady, dull drone. He didn't mind walking in the rain
and his stride was somewhat casual as he walked north
on Wharf Street. But later, on Vernon, the anxiety hit
him again and he hurried his pace.

Entering the house, he quickly checked all the rooms.
Frank was nowhere around, Tom and Lola were asleep,
and Bella's room was empty. He went into the unlit
parlor, took a chair near the window, and sat there in
the dark waiting for Bella to come home.

Some nights Bella came home very late. Maybe
tonight she wouldn't be coming home at all. Maybe she
was on a bus or a train, telling herself she'd evened the
score and it was a wise move now to get out of town. But
while the thought drifted through his mind, he saw Bella

walking across Vernon Street and approaching the house. She moved somewhat unsteadily. She wasn't really drunk, but it was obvious she'd been drinking.

He stood away from the window. The door opened and Bella came in and plumped herself on the sofa. In the darkness of the parlor she didn't see him, but enough light came through the window so that he could watch what she was doing. Her handbag was open and she was taking out a pack of cigarettes. She put one in her mouth and then she searched for a match.

Kerrigan spoke very softly. "Hello, Bella."

She let out a startled cry.

"It's only me," he said. He flicked the wall switch, and the ceiling bulbs were lit.

Bella sat stiffly, holding her breath as she stared at him. It seemed that her eyes were coming out of her face.

Kerrigan moved toward her. He had a match book in his hand. He struck a match and applied the flame to her cigarette, but she didn't inhale. He kept the flame there and finally she took a spasmodic drag, her body shaking as the smoke came out of her mouth.

He blew out the match, dropped it into a tray. Then very slowly, as though he were performing a carefully rehearsed ceremony, he reached into his trousers pocket and took out the folded money, the two fives and the ten. He unfolded the bills and smoothed them between his fingers. Then he extended them slowly and held them in front of her bulging eyes.

She was trying to look at something else, trying to stare at the carpet, a chair, the wall, anything at all, just so she wouldn't be seeing the money. But although her head moved, her eyes were fastened on the money.

"Here," he said, offering her the money. "It's yours."

He waited for her to take the bills. She kept her hands down, her fingers gripping the edge of the sofa. Her throat contracted as though she were trying to swallow something very thick and heavy in her throat.

Then suddenly her shoulders sagged. She lowered her head. "Oh, my God," she moaned. "Oh, my God."

Kerrigan placed the bills in the opened handbag. He said, "Don't take it so hard. You haven't lost anything. After all, you got your money back."

She looked at him. "Why don't you do it?"

"Do what?"

"Knock my teeth out. Break my neck."

He shook his head. He said, "I think you're hurt enough already."

She dragged at the cigarette. Then she leaned back heavily against the sofa pillow, gazing past him and saying dully, "How'd you get the money?"

He shrugged. "I asked for it."

She went on gazing past him. "I should have known they'd louse things up." For a long moment she was quiet. And then, as though she were very tired, she closed her eyes. "All right, tell me what happened."

"Nothing much. But they made a nice try. They came damn near earning their pay."

She looked at his hands. His knuckles were skinned and she nodded slowly and said, "It musta been a nice little party."

"Yeah," he said dryly, "it was a lot of fun."

"They get banged up much?"

"Enough to make it a sad ending," he said. "One of them is out of business for at least a month. The other one is out for keeps."

She took another drag at the cigarette. She didn't say anything.

He said, "Next time you hire a wrecking crew, don't pay them in advance."

The smoke drifted very slowly from her lips. Her eyes followed the uncurling tendrils as she said, "It wasn't me who paid them. And it wasn't my idea to hire them."

He seized her shoulders. "What was the setup?"

Her lips were locked tightly. She started to shake her head.

"Cut that out," he said. "You've started to tell me and you're gonna finish."

"I can't."

"But you will." His grip on her shoulders was like a set of metal clamps. "I had a feeling it wasn't your idea to begin with. It figures there was an agent in charge of this deal. It figures from every angle. There's someone in this neighborhood who knows I'm looking for him. He knows what's gonna happen when I find out who he is and get my hands on him. You check what I'm talkin' about?"

Bella blinked several times. Her mouth opened but no sound came through.

"I'm talkin' about my sister," he said. "She killed herself because she was jumped and ruined and driven crazy. Whoever he is, he knows I'll keep looking until I find him. So it stands to reason he don't want me around. You check it now?"

She stopped squirming. She stared at him.

He said, "The man is nervous. He's scared. What he'd like most is to see me in a wooden box. But he'd probably settle for less, like a twenty-dollar deal to cripple me. To put me out of action so he'd be safe for a while. And that's where you come in."

She shut her eyes tightly.

He kept the tight hold on her shoulders. "The way it lines up," he said, "you were used for sucker bait. The man knew you had it in for me. He appointed himself as a friendly adviser. Tells you there's a way to even the score, and before you know what you're doing, you give him the twenty dollars. Ain't that how it happened?"

She nodded dazedly.

Kerrigan went on, "He hands the money to the hooligans. He tells them you're the customer. That keeps his name out of it, just in case there's a slip-up. Anyway, that's what he thought. But you know his name and I'm waiting for you to open your mouth."

"No." She choked on it. "Don't make me tell."

"Come on," he gritted. His hands put more pressure on her shoulders.

She winced. His fingers burned into her flesh and there were pain and fear in her eyes. Yet it wasn't at all like physical pain. And it seemed the fear was more for him than for herself.

Then all at once there was nothing in her eyes. Her voice was toneless as she said, "It was Frank."

Then it was quiet in the parlor. But he had a feeling the room was moving. It was like a chamber on wheels going away from everything, falling off the edge of the world.

He took his hands away from her shoulders. He turned away from her, and heard himself saying, "As if I didn't know."

Bella had her head lowered. Her hands covered her face.

"Well," he said, "it adds up. The twenty dollars was the one thing he needed. He never has a nickel in his pockets."

She spoke in a broken whisper. "I should have guessed what was in his mind. But I couldn't think straight. I was half crazy. Or maybe crazy all the way. I just wanted to see you get hurt."

"He knew that," Kerrigan said. "He knew it wouldn't be no trouble to sell you a bill of goods."

She was quiet for some moments. And then, in a lower whisper, "I came near spending more than the twenty."

"Did he ask for more?"

"He wanted me to spend a hundred."

He turned and looked at her. "Why didn't you?"

Bella stared at the carpet. "I didn't have it."

"Did he tell you what a hundred would buy?"

"He said it would put you in a grave."

Kerrigan breathed in slowly. He thought, This is worse than a grave, worse than hell.

Then gradually his mouth hardened. His arms were stiff at his sides. "All right," he said. "Where is he?"

She raised her head. She looked at him and saw something in his eyes that made her go cold.

"You don't hafta tell me," he said. "I'll find him."

He moved toward the door. His hand was on the door-knob when Bella leaped from the sofa, ran to him, and grabbed his arms.

"No," she gasped. "No, don't."

"Let go."

"Please don't," she begged. "Stay here for a while. Think it over."

He tried to pull away from her. "I said let go."

She was using all her strength to drag him away from the door. "I won't letcha," she said. "You'll only do something you'll be sorry for."

Her grip was like iron. Now she had her arms wrapped

around his middle and he could hardly breathe. "Goddamn you," he wheezed. "You gonna let go?"

"No," she said. "You gotta listen."

"I've listened enough. I've heard all I need to know."

"You know what'll happen if you go out that door?"

Instead of answering, he gave her a vicious jab
with his elbow. It caught her in the side and she groaned.
But she wouldn't release her hold on him. He jabbed
her again as she went on dragging him backward. She
grunted and held him more tightly. It was as though she
wanted him to keep jabbing her, to take it out on her.

"If you don't let go," he hissed, "you're gonna get hurt."

"Go ahead and hurt me. You got both arms free."

"You're askin' for grief."

Her breath came in grinding sobs. "I'm askin' you to
listen, that's all. Just listen to me. I want you to go in
your room and pack your things. And then I'll walk you
to the streetcar. You'll take that ride uptown. And you'll
stay there. With her."

His arms fell limply at his sides.

Bella relaxed her hold just a little. "Will you do it?"

He was looking at the door. He didn't say anything.

"Please do it," Bella said. "Go to her and live with her
and never come back here. Don't even use the phone. Or
write. Just forget about all this. Forget you ever lived in
this house."

"You make it sound easy."

"Sure it's easy. You said so yourself. Just a matter of
spending the carfare." Her voice was torn with a sob.
"Fifteen cents."

"That's cheap enough," he said. "Maybe it's too cheap. I
think it costs more than that to break off all connections."

Then slowly, gently, he took hold of her wrists, he

unfastened her arms from around his middle. She didn't look at him as she stepped away, giving him an un-impeded path to the door. But as he heard the sound of the doorknob turning, she made one last try to hold him back, calling on the only power that could stop him now, moaning, "Dear God, don't let him do it."

But the door was already open. Bella sank to her knees, weeping without sound. Through the window she saw him as he stepped down off the doorstep. His face was like something carved from rock, a profile of hardened whiteness, very white against the darkness of the street. Then he was crossing Vernon and she saw the route he was taking. He moved along a diagonal path aiming at a foggy yellow glow in the distance, the window of Dugan's Den.

CHAPTER 16

As he entered the taproom he heard voices and saw faces
but everything was a blur that didn't seem real and had
no meaning. His eyes were lenses going past the faces
and searching for Frank. But Frank wasn't there. He
told himself to stand near the door and wait. And just
then someone yelled, "Come join the party."

It was the voice of the skinny hag, Dora. She sat with
several others at a couple of tables pushed together for
what seemed like a celebration. Kerrigan focused on the
drinkers. Dora was seated between Mooney and Nick
Andros. The other chairs were occupied by the humpbacked wino and Newton Channing. Next to Channing
there was an empty chair and the person who'd been
sitting on it was prone on the floor, face down and out
cold. He looked at the sleeper and saw the orange hair
and shapeless figure of Dora's friend Frieda.

For some moments he stood there gazing down at
Frieda. She had one arm outstretched and he saw something that glittered on her finger. It was a very large
green stone and he didn't need to be told it was
artificial.

Dora said, "It cost a goddamn fortune." She reached
across the table to nudge Channing's arm. "Go on, tell
him how much it cost."

"Three-ninety-five," Channing said.

"You hear?" Dora screeched at Kerrigan. Then again

she nudged Channing. "Now tell him what it's for. Tell him why we're celebrating."

"Gladly," Channing said. He stood up ceremoniously. He was wearing a clean white shirt and a straw-colored linen suit. His face was solemn as he bowed to the sleeping woman on the floor. Then he bowed to Kerrigan and said, "Welcome to our little gathering. It's an engagement party."

"You're goddamn right it is," Dora hollered. She reached through a maze of bottles and glasses and found a water glass containing gin. Lifting the glass, she tried to rise for a toast and couldn't make it to her feet. She leaned heavily against Mooney, spilling some gin on his shoulder as she pronounced a toast for all the world to hear:

"The yellow moon may kiss the sky, The bees may kiss the butterfly, The morning dew may kiss the grass, And you, my friends—"

"Knock it off," Nick Andros cut in. He pointed to the empty chair and shouted to Kerrigan, "Come on and sit down and have a drink."

Kerrigan didn't move. "I'm looking for my brother," he said. "Anyone here seen my brother?"

"The hell with your brother," Nick said.

"The hell with everybody," Dora yelled. "The yellow moon may kiss the sky—"

"Will you kindly shut up?" Nick requested. He kept beckoning Kerrigan to take the empty chair.

Kerrigan looked at Mooney. "You seen him?"

Mooney shook his head slowly. His eyes were half closed and he looked drunk. But he was studying

Kerrigan's face and gradually his mouth opened, his eyes widened, and he sat up straight and stiffly. He tried not to take it further than that, but his hands were lifted and then came down hard on the table and a bottle fell off the edge and crashed to the floor. At the table all talk was stopped. The only sound in the room was the squeaky tune coming from behind the bar. Kerrigan looked in that direction and saw Dugan standing with his arms folded, his eyes closed, humming the melody that took him away from Vernon Street.

Moving toward the bar, Kerrigan said, "Hey, Dugan."

Dugan opened his eyes. The humming slowed down just a little.

"My brother been here?" Kerrigan asked.

Dugan shook his head. Then his eyes were closed again and he picked up the tempo of the tune.

A hand touched Kerrigan's arm. He turned and saw Mooney. The sign painter's face was expressionless.

"Is this what I think it is?" Mooney asked quietly.

Kerrigan pulled his arm away from Mooney's hand. "Go back to the table."

Mooney didn't move. He said, "Why don't you tell me?"

"It don't concern you." But then he remembered the water-color portrait in Mooney's room. He gazed past Mooney and said, "Well, I guess you got a right to know. I've been putting some facts together and finally got the answer."

Mooney just stood there and waited.

Kerrigan closed his eyes for a moment. He heard himself saying, "The creep who jumped my sister was her own brother."

"No," Mooney said. "Don't tell me that. You can't tell me that."

"But I am telling you."

"You know what you're saying?"

Kerrigan nodded.

"You sure?" Mooney's voice quivered just a little. "You absolutely sure?"

"I got it all summed up," Kerrigan said. "It checks."

"You have proof?"

"I know what I need to know. That's enough." He looked down at his hands. His fingers were distended, bent stiffly, like claws.

Mooney said, "We got some hundred proof on the table. I'll fix you a double shot."

"No," Kerrigan said. "I don't want that. All I want is to see him walking in here."

"Now look, Bill—"

But Kerrigan wasn't looking or listening. He wasn't feeling the urgent grip that Mooney put on his arms. He spoke in a choked whisper, saying, "Gonna wait here for him. He'll show. And when he does—"

"Bill, for God's sake!"

"Gonna put him where he put her. Gonna put him in a casket."

And then again everything was a blur. He heard a jumble of noises coming from the table where Nick Andros was telling Dora to shut up and Newton Channing laughed lightly at some comment from the hump-backed wino. From behind the bar the humming sound of Dugan's tune provided vague background music for the clinking of glasses and the drinkers' voices. It went on and on like that, with Mooney's voice begging him to come to the table and have the double shot, and his own voice telling Mooney to leave him alone. Then suddenly he heard a sound that wasn't

glass on glass or glass on tabletop or anyone's spoken
words. It was the sound of the door as someone came in
from the street.

He turned his head and saw his brother.

He heard himself making a noise that was like air
coming out from a collapsed balloon.

And after that there was no sound at all. Not even
from Dugan.

The quiet stretched as a rubber band stretches and
finally can't stretch any more and the fibers split apart.
In that instant, as he moved, he sensed Mooney's hands
trying to hold him back and his arm was a scythe making
contact with the sign painter's ribs.

Mooney sailed halfway across the room, came up
against a table, sailed over it and took a chair with him
as he went to the floor. Then Mooney tried to get up and
he couldn't get up. He was resting on his side with all
the breath knocked out of his body. He saw Kerrigan
lunging at Frank, and Kerrigan's hands taking hold of
Frank's throat.

"I can't let you live," Kerrigan said. "I can't."

Frank's eyes bulged. His face was getting blue.

"Your own sister," Kerrigan said. "You ruined your
own sister." And then, to everyone in the room, to every
unseen face beyond the room, "How can I let him live?"

He squeezed harder. There was a gurgling noise. But
it wasn't coming from Frank. It came from his own
throat, as though he was crushing his own flesh, stop-
ping the flow of his own blood. He told himself to close
his eyes, he didn't want to watch what he was doing.
But his eyes wouldn't close and he was seeing the con-
vulsive movement of Frank's gaping mouth. He realized
that Frank was trying to tell him something.

His fingers reduced the pressure. He heard Frank gasping, "I didn't do it."

He released the hold. Frank was on his knees, trying to cough, trying to talk, making gagging sounds that gradually gave way to sighs.

"Talk," Kerrigan gritted. "Talk fast."

"I didn't do it," Frank repeated. "I swear I didn't."

For some moments there was no sound in the room. Yet in the stillness there was the feeling of something racing through the air, whirling around and around to turn everything upside down.

Frank was lifting himself from the floor. He staggered sideways and leaned heavily against the bar. His eyes were shut tightly and he had his knuckles pressed against his temples.

"You gonna talk?" Kerrigan demanded.

But Frank didn't hear. He seemed to be alone with himself. Then gradually his eyes opened and he was staring up at the ceiling. His hands were lowered, his arms loose at his sides. He spoke to whatever he saw there on the ceiling. "It's straight now," he whispered. "I finally got it straight."

Then it was quiet again. Kerrigan had his mouth open but he couldn't speak. He was trying to get hold of his thoughts, the hollow thoughts that wouldn't add and wouldn't fit and had him trapped somewhere between icy rage and the misty abyss of puzzlement.

And finally he heard Frank saying, "It comes back. All of it. Comes back on all four wheels."

"Spill it."

Frank's voice was level and calm. "The night it happened I was plastered. Couldn't remember where I went or what I did. And all these months it's been like that, getting worse and worse until it reached the point where I gave up trying. I told myself it was me who did it. I really believed it was me."

Kerrigan spoke slowly, the sound edging through his tightened lips. "You sure it wasn't you? You absolutely sure?"

"It couldn't be me," Frank said. And then, completely certain of what he was saying, not trying to force it, just saying it because it was true, "I spent that night in a joint on Second Street. Went in before dark and didn't come out till the next afternoon."

Kerrigan's eyes narrowed. He was studying Frank's face.

Frank said, "I been sick with this thing a long time. It's been like a spike jabbing into my head. I ain't been able to sleep, and couldn't eat, and there were times I could hardly breathe."

Kerrigan didn't say anything. He could feel the truth coming out of Frank's eyes.

He heard Frank saying, "A spike in my head, that's what it was. And every time you looked at me, that spike went in deeper. As if you were telling me what I was telling myself. It got so bad I couldn't take it any more."

"Is that why you hired the gorillas?"

Frank nodded. "I musta gone haywire, just crazy enough to want you out of the way. Musta figured the only way to get rid of that spike was to use it on you."

Kerrigan took a deep breath. It was more like a sigh, as though a tremendous weight had been eased off his chest.

Frank said, "You sure as hell choked it outta me." He grinned weakly and rubbed his throat. "You squeezed just hard enough to loosen that spike. So now it's out."

Kerrigan smiled. He put his hand on Frank's shoulder. Frank grinned at him with a mouth that didn't twitch and eyes that weren't glazed.

"I'm all right now," Frank said. "You see the way it is? I'm really all right now."

Kerrigan nodded. He gazed past Frank. The smile gradually faded from his lips as he thought of Catherine. And he was saying to himself, You still don't know who did it.

And then, very slowly, he felt the answer coming.

He stood there and told himself he was getting the answer. He knew it had no connection with any man's face or any man's name. His eyes were focused through the window facing Vernon Street. He peered out past the murky glass and saw the moonlight reflected on the jutting cobblestones. It was a yellow-green glow drifting across Vernon and forming pools of light in the gutter. He saw it glimmering on the rutted sidewalk and going on and on toward all the dark alleys where countless creatures of the night played hide-and-seek.

And no matter where the weaker ones were hiding, they'd never get away from the Vernon moon. It had them trapped. It had them doomed. Sooner or later they'd be mauled and battered and crushed. They'd learn the hard way that Vernon Street was no place for delicate bodies or timid souls. They were prey, that was all, they were destined for the maw of the ever hungry eater, the Vernon gutter.

He stared out at the moonlit street. Without sound he said, You did it to Catherine. You.

It was as though the street could hear. He sensed that it was making a jeering reply. A raucous voice seemed to say, So what? So watcha gonna do about it?

And the street went on jeering, saying, Your sister couldn't take it, and the same goes for you. And it chose that moment to display its hole card. It opened the door of Dugan's Den and showed him the golden-haired dream girl from uptown. As he stared at Loretta, he could hear the street saying, Well, here she is. She's come to take your hand and lift you from the gutter.

Loretta was walking toward him. Something quivered in his brain and he thought, She reminds me of someone. And then it was there, the memory of the hopes he'd had for Catherine and himself, the hopes he'd lost in a dark alley and yearned to find again.

But taproom noises interfered. Two dimes clinked on the table as Dugan poured a drink for Frank. At the table Nick Andros poured gin for Dora. "Say when," Nick said. But Dora said nothing, for gin had no connection with time. As the gin splashed over the edge of the glass, Kerrigan looked toward the table. He saw Frieda getting up from the floor. Mooney was doing the same, and they almost bumped heads as they came to their feet. Then Frieda staggered backward and bumped the humpbacked wino off his chair. Channing caught hold of Frieda and tried to steady her and she said, "Let go, goddamnit, I can stand on my own two legs." There was a shout of approval from Dora. It inspired Frieda to a further statement of policy. She said to Channing, "Don't put yer hands on me unless I tell you to."

Channing shrugged, preferring to let it go at that. But Nick Andros frowned and expressed the male point of view, saying, "You're wearing his engagement ring, he's your fiance." Frieda blinked, looked down at the ring on her finger, and then with some energetic twisting she pulled it off. For some moments she seemed reluctant to part with the green stone. She held the ring tightly, frowning at it. Then suddenly she placed the ring on the table in front of Channing. Her voice was quiet as she

said, "Take it back to where you got it. This pussycat's a
self-supporting individual."

For a moment Channing just sat there with nothing
in his eyes as he thought it over. Then, with another
shrug, he lowered the ring into his jacket pocket. So that
took care of that, and then he was smiling at Frieda and
saying, "Have a drink?"

Frieda nodded emphatically. She sat down beside him
and watched him pour the gin. She lifted the glass and
said loudly, "This juice is all I need from any man. Even
if he wears clean shirts." But then, as though using her
right hand to make up for a left-handed swipe, she patted
the side of Channing's head and spoke in a softer tone.
"Don't take it to heart, sweetie. You're really cute. It's
nice to sit here and drink with you. But that's as far as
we can take it. After all, it's every cat to his own alley."

So true, Kerrigan thought. He looked at Loretta, who
stood there waiting for him to say something. His eyes
aimed down to what she had on her finger, the hinged
ring from the Greek's loose-leaf notebook. His brain said,
No dice. She'll hafta take it off. And his heart ached as
he gazed at her face. Her face told him that she knew
what he was thinking and her own heart was aching.

He said, "I'll have a talk with the Greek. He'll get rid
of the license. All he has to do is light a match."

She didn't say anything. She looked at the ring on her
finger. She started to take it off and it wanted to stay
there, as though it were a part of her that pleaded not to
be torn away.

He said, "It'll come off. Just loosen the hinge."

Her eyes were wet. "If we could only—"

"But we can't," he said. "Don't you see the way it is?
We don't ride the same track. I can't live your kind of

life and you can't live mine. It ain't anyone's fault. It's just the way the cards are stacked."

She nodded slowly. And just then the ring came off. It dropped from her limp hand and rolled across the floor and went under the bar to vanish in the darkness of all lost dreams. He heard the final tinkling sound it made, a plaintive little sound that accompanied her voice saying good-by. Then there was the sound of his own footsteps walking out of Dugan's Den.

As he came off the pavement to cross the Vernon cobblestones, his tread was heavy, coming down solidly on solid ground. He moved along with a deliberate stride that told each stone it was there to be stepped on, and he damn well knew how to walk this street, how to handle every bump and rut and hole in the gutter. He went past them all, and went up on the doorstep of the house where he lived. As he pushed open the door, it suddenly occurred to him that he was damned hungry.

In the parlor, Bella was lying face down on the sofa. He gave her a slap on her rump. "Get up," he said. "Make me some supper."

**Also by David Goodis and published
by Serpent's Tail**

The BLONDE on the STREET CORNER

'She took a final drag at the cigarette, flipped it away, and said, "I don't get this line of talk. It's way over my head. I think you have been reading fairy-tales, or something. Maybe you're waiting for some dream girl to come along in a coach drawn by six white horses, and she'll pick you up and haul you away to the clouds, where it's all milk and honey and springtime all year around. Maybe that's what you're waiting for. That dream girl."

"Maybe," he murmured. And then he looked at the blonde. His smile was soft and friendly and he said, "I guess that's why I can't start with you. I'm waiting for the dream girl."

But the dream girl does not come. In the meantime Ralph must deal with the yearnings of everyday life and take what he is offered.

Written in 1954, *The Blonde on the Street Corner* is full of the passions and desires that are the hallmarks of a David Goodis novel.

'His books are a lethally potent cocktail of surreal description, brilliant language, cracker barrel philosophy and gripping obsession.' Adrian Wootton